TALL and PROUD

By Vian Smith

The First Thunder
Genesis Down
Green Heart
Martin Rides the Moor
Pride of the Moor
A Second Chance
Tall and Proud

TALL and PROUD

VIAN SMITH

Illustrated by Don Stivers

DOUBLEDAY & COMPANY, INC., GARDEN CITY, NEW YORK

Library of Congress Catalog Card Number AC 67–10049
Copyright © 1966 by Vian Smith
All Rights Reserved
Printed in the United States of America

For Seychelles who won many hurdle races and steeplechases and who earned the nickname "King Sam"

TALL and PROUD

CHAPTER ONE

Gail looked from the window and it was there. Tall and proud, as high on the hill as a king. It seemed to be a dream come true, but the story of Gail and the dream come true did not begin there.

It began one day in May, when she was playing in the moorland stream.

The game she was playing was elaborate. Only she could understand it, because it was her invention and she reserved the right to change it without bothering to explain or to make it sensible to a mere boy like Rod.

Rod Jennings was her nearest neighbor. They played together sometimes because neither had anybody else, but usually they quarreled because Rod called her "Windy" and asked too many questions.

He asked too many questions that afternoon in the stream. He stood on the bank and looked at her pile of stones in a scornful way and looked at the bits of wood which were supposed to be ships and asked what all the nattering was about.

A silly question, for of course the pile of stones was an island, although at first it had been a dam. And of course the ships were galleons, wrecked by a mighty storm and sinking with all hands until she plunged into the heaving sea and rescued them and brought them to her island.

"There's been a storm," Gail said, grabbing a small celluloid doll as it floated past.

But you couldn't explain. You spoiled it if you tried to convince others that the celluloid dolls were Marie Antoinette, who wasn't really beheaded at all, and John the Baptist who wasn't either. You could only wade to the island and decide on the way that this doll wasn't Captain Hornblower, as you had intended. It was the Archbishop of Canterbury, who had been going around the world on a peace mission and who would almost certainly have the other survivors building a church in five minutes.

"Who?" Rod said.

Gail recognized his disbelieving voice. She placed the Archbishop on a high rock, from which he could lead the survivors in "Lift Up Your Hearts."

"He's got a hole in," Rod protested.

She knew that. It explained the very interesting slopping sound which the Archbishop made. It also explained why this little doll was among her favorites; for the hole always became a wound and the bandaging gave her a chance to be Florence Nightingale. She asked the Archbishop to wait a minute and waded back for the Beatles; saving Ringo first because he was the most important.

"Who are you now?" Rod asked.

"Gulliver," Gail answered, although it should have been obvious.

"Yah," Rod said in disgust. Then he added "Windy," and after a while he said "Girls" because the nickname was not derisive enough. Yet he did not move away. He stayed on the bank, frowning with all his freckles. He didn't say anything, but just being there was enough.

Her elaborate adventures became just a silly game which only a girl would invent.

Gail tried to cling to her belief, turning the Archbishop of Canterbury into Prince Charles to give the story a surprising twist. But you couldn't be Gulliver one minute and Florence Nightingale the next with a red-haired critic scowling on the bank.

"What's the time?" Gail asked.

"Dunno," Rod said.

"Goodness, is it that late?" She prepared to abandon her game, making the time an excuse because no boy must think he could put her off. "My mother will be mad."

She gathered the nine small dolls which played so many parts in her games. It was then that she began to feel the strange pain in her head, the dizziness, the stiffness at the back of her neck. She thought she had been wading too long in cold water; that she'd be all right as soon as she reached the bank and found her socks and became Gail Fleming again.

So she splashed to the bank and sat to dry her feet with a handkerchief. Rod watched in disgust; although she could see nothing wrong in drying your feet with a handkerchief. Unless you happened to be an adult and fussy about such things.

"You ought to do it with dry grass," Rod said. "That's how the pioneers did it in the Wild West."

Rod was an expert on the Wild West and steeplechase racing. He knew more about Billy the Kid and the Grand National than he did about the Battle of Hastings.

"Well, bully for the pioneers," Gail said.

It was a brave gesture, for the pain in her head was worse. When she looked at Rod to see if he had noticed, his outline was vague, like a photograph out of focus.

Of course Rod hadn't noticed. He pulled a face when

she put on socks and shoes, for a real country girl wouldn't bother with either. Cheyenne squaws had gone bare foot, hadn't they? Never squawking about stones or prickles or what their mothers would say. He said, "Where're you off?"

"Home," Gail said.

Rod made a scornful sound, as though there were much better places to go if only he could think of them. Then he moved away, hands in pockets and whistling. It was a thoughtful whistle, a sure sign that he was drifting into his own favorite game; when he ceased to be Rod Jennings, freckled son of a forester and bottom of 2B at the last day of reckoning. He became Wyatt Earp in Dodge City, walking the middle of the dust street with the fastest guns watching slit-eyed from the sidewalks.

"Yah, boys," Gail said.

But even to her own ears the taunt did not seem real. It came from somebody else, making her two people. It seemed that she was the girl who knew about Dodge City and 2B and could stand up for herself against any boy. At the same time she was a frail little person, who couldn't see properly or stand up properly, who was frightened by the wobbling in her legs.

She had only one idea; to get home before this strange feeling, whatever it was, dragged her down so that she gave in to sleep. She crossed the wilderness of heather and bracken, recognizing the trees which showed where her father's land began. But her legs would not hurry. Her eyes would not look up. She saw only the ground immediately ahead and did not realize that her mother was coming out.

"Gail," Mrs. Fleming said, "what's the matter?"

Gail tried to shake her head, to deny that there was anything the matter. But she leaned into her mother as the arm came around and suddenly she was crying, without realizing why or feeling any pain.

"Out too long," Mrs. Fleming said. "In the sun too long."

That was the explanation given to Mr. Fleming when he came home in the evening. He was a journalist and worked for a weekly newspaper in the market town five miles away. He came in and threw his hat anywhere, the way he always did. Then he looked around for Gail and Mrs. Fleming said, "Not very well. I put her to bed."

Instantly he was alarmed, but Mrs. Fleming tried to reassure. They went up the twisting staircase to Gail's bedroom. The door was open. She was asleep. But it didn't seem a peaceful sleep. There was a pucker between her eyebrows.

John Fleming darted a glance to his wife, but she didn't seem especially worried. So he said nothing because he might be wrong and family friends always teased him about Gail. You'd think she was the only girl in the world, they said. You make every cold as bad as pneumonia.

"She'll be all right," Mrs. Fleming said. "A good sleep can do wonders."

Still John Fleming hesitated, looking at his daughter and wondering what was going on in that troubled silence where he could not help her. Then he remembered that his working day was not over. He had time only to snatch a quick meal, then hurry back to the market town and to a meeting of moorland farmers.

It was a long meeting; all about farm prices and subsidies and what the Government ought to do. John Fleming took in shorthand what seemed to be important, but at the back of his mind he was still thinking of his daughter.

That's why he knew what it was when the chairman

interrupted the meeting to say, "There's a phone call for Mr. Fleming of the *Weekly Advertiser*. They say it's urgent."

John Fleming knew it must be. He was up from the reporters' table at once, almost knocking it over in his haste to get out to the hall where the telephone was. Common sense kept telling him that it could be anybody, his editor perhaps; but he knew whose the voice would be and what it would say.

"John," Mrs. Fleming said.

"Yes."

"It's Gail. We mustn't get frightened, but it's more than just a headache."

"What happened since I left?"

"She woke up about an hour ago." Barbara Fleming stopped, squeezing the fright out of her voice. "But it wasn't really waking up. A sort of delirium. Very hot and feverish. I took her temperature. Nearly 103."

John Fleming took another grip on the telephone. His hands were so hot that the bakelite was slippery. His fingers left great prints on it.

"The doctor," he said. "You shouldn't have rung me, Barbara. Not before the doctor."

"I rang Dr. Barlow first," Mrs. Fleming said. "He's on his way."

"So am I," John Fleming said. "I'll be there in fifteen minutes."

It seemed much longer; for at first the shabby car wouldn't start and when it did, the old engine wouldn't go fast enough up the Dartmoor hills. He drove grimly, blaming himself because he should have seen it, then consoling himself because in the morning it might be all right.

The doctor was there and John Fleming knew from one

glance at his face that it would not be all right. He stood in the doorway, breathless from the stairs, watching Dr. Barlow feel Gail's pulse and forehead, then put his clasped hands behind her head and lift. She opened her mouth in a silent cry.

The doctor unclasped his hands immediately and for a long moment the only sound in the room was Gail's hot breathing. Then she twisted her head from side to side and began to talk; an incoherent mumble that made no sense.

John Fleming thought he heard the word "Gulliver." Then several times he recognized "Topper." He glanced to his wife, and Barbara Fleming said, "She was talking about Topper just now. In her delirium."

The father thought, she's living it all again; the day when Topper, her chestnut pony, had found a clipping of yew from somebody's hedge and had eaten it and had trotted on for perhaps a mile before falling. Dead. As suddenly as that.

Gail had been ten years old and had waited two hours beside her dead pony until somebody had found her on the lonely road and telephoned her parents and her father had come with a lorry to take away the terrible thing.

Her parents had agreed that she must never have another pet, for every pet must be a risk. They had watched her carefully in the months which followed, hoping that she'd get over it and would forget and wouldn't call to Topper in her dreams. They had thought, hoped, that she'd found escape in those fantasies which made sense to no one except herself. Now they knew how little she had forgotten. She was living it again in the red world of delirium.

Dr. Barlow turned from the bed, pretending to be casual. "Well, we must get her to hospital."

"What's wrong?" Mrs. Fleming asked.

But the doctor didn't answer. He said, "If I can use your phone."

"Of course." Mrs. Fleming led the way down the stairs. "It's in the hall."

John Fleming didn't follow them. He stayed near his daughter's bed, kneeling beside her, his hand flinching when it touched her forehead. He was trying to get through to her; to assure her that she was safe. At the same time he was listening to the doctor, telephoning first for an ambulance, then to a hospital in the city. John Fleming recognized the name of the hospital. Astonished, he thought, but that's for isolation cases. He straightened from the bed. He moved to the landing. Slowly he went down the stairs.

The doctor looked up to the father coming down. He said, "It can be sudden." But he did not say what could be sudden and before either parent could press for more, he suggested that Mrs. Fleming pack a case. Toothpaste, toothbrush, sponge, dressing gown. Gail would need them and packing would give the mother something to do.

Mrs. Fleming turned to the stairs. They watched her go up, then heard her opening drawers and crossing the landing to the bathroom. John Fleming looked back to the doctor and after a while Dr. Barlow looked at him.

Quietly he said, "Don't tell your wife."

John Fleming waited to hear what he must not tell his wife.

"You might have to burn all the things in her room. Especially the books."

John Fleming was sure then, but could not believe it.

He waited for the doctor to put it into words, and after a while the doctor said, "I'm very afraid it's polio."

"But Gail has been vaccinated. She couldn't have polio."

"Nothing is one hundred percent foolproof," the doctor responded.

CHAPTER TWO

Gail began to awaken. She knew without opening her eyes that she'd been taken somewhere. There were haphazard memories of being carried downstairs; of traveling by ambulance with her father sitting near and of a nurse bending over. She remembered voices in the yard and the driver calling "Emergency" and doors opening and footsteps coming around to help with the stretcher.

Being carried on a stretcher had given her a strange feeling of unreality; like lying on a magic carpet, with the carpet rising and moving and knowing the way. You had to go wherever the carpet decided.

She'd tried to think of this magic carpet and to wonder where it was taking her and why and how soon she would be home again. But the effort of concentration had been too much and she had slipped back to unconsciousness. Now she was coming out of darkness.

She opened her eyes and had an impression of whiteness; of figures in white coats watching. But her eyes would not stay open. The lids fell before she could see if her father was there.

She slept what seemed five minutes but might have been five hours, and when she opened her eyes again the figures in white were still there. She thought, like umpires. Like cricket umpires on the school field.

Then she noticed something else. Each was masked. The masks covered the lower part of their faces and suddenly the men were robbers. A gang of robbers, come to steal the seven shillings and eight pence which she had saved for her father's birthday.

But she believed that only for a second. Then she was laughing in her head because of course they weren't robbers. The masks were surgical masks, covering nose and mouth to prevent infection. The men were doctors.

She looked at the eyes which were different from the others; older and more intent, watching her without blinking. She tried to say, "I thought you were Dick Turpin."

The doctor moved toward her. He said, "Hullo, little girl," and Gail wanted to answer that. She wasn't little. She was almost as old as Rod Jennings and nearly as tall, too.

The doctor felt her pulse, her forehead. One of the younger doctors gave him a piece of board with a strong clip at the top. Gail could not see the chart, but guessed that it was clipped to the board and that the chart recorded in figures and red dots what the hospital needed to know.

He studied the chart a minute, then looked at Gail again. His eyes were gray. She wanted to ask, "Where's my father?" But the words wouldn't come. She tried again but still they wouldn't. They were only in her head.

The doctor guessed what her eyes were trying to say. The mask went in and out as he said, "Your father and mother will be here as soon as you're strong enough."

That seemed ridiculous, for you don't need to be strong to see your parents. She tried to explain that she felt fine and what was she doing here and how long had she been asleep?

"They come every day," the doctor said. "To the window there."

He pointed but Gail could not move her head.

"They can't come in, so they stand at the window. When you're strong enough we'll put the bed near."

Gail kept her eyes on him but she was only half listening to what he said. She was thinking of that pain when she had tried to move her head. She tried again, furtively, without the men noticing. Again it came, sharp enough to frighten.

The fright showed in her eyes and the doctor said, "There's nothing to be afraid of. My name is Craig, Dr. Craig. And if there's anything you are afraid of, you just tell me." The gray eyes smiled. "We'll soon put it right, whatever it is."

Gail answered the smile, not because she believed what he said but because he expected it.

"You're not strong enough to talk." Dr. Craig touched her lightly, reassuringly. "Just sleep a while longer."

So Gail slept and did not know that her parents had long talks with Dr. Craig about how it might have happened. Neither did she know that public health officials were on Dartmoor, taking samples of the stream and examining them for pollution. All her books were destroyed. Her room was sealed and fumigated. Meanwhile form teachers warned pupils and parents that one case of polio had been confirmed and that every care must be taken to avert an outbreak. Everyone looked at Rod Jennings, making him the most likely victim.

Rod was embarrassed by such attention. He had to stand still and answer questions: had he waded in the stream, had he felt a stiffness in his neck or dizziness or headaches? He had to promise that if ever he felt any of the early symptoms, he would tell form teacher or parents or the driver of the school bus if the symptoms began on the journey home.

"It can be very sudden," a public health official warned him. "Look what happened to poor Gail."

Rod didn't confide what he thought of "poor Gail." Trust a girl to let something like this happen. Trust Windy Fleming to stop him fishing in that stream.

After a while Gail could keep her eyes open long enough to see where she was; in what seemed to be a glass ward, with glass walls on three sides through which nurses and doctors could watch her as they passed along the corridors. On the fourth side was a big window which looked out on the hospital gardens. She wanted to laugh. She thought, like a goldfish in a bowl. But behind the laugh was fright, because this must be the hospital in the city and only serious cases were taken to the city.

Her bed had been moved near the window. She could look out without hurting her head. So she looked out and tried to imagine what day it was, what time it was, and what her parents might be doing now.

If it was Friday and eleven o'clock her mother would be in the market town shopping for the weekend, while her father would be in that newspaper office which smelled of ink and dust; getting ratty as he always did on a Friday because Friday was press day, when the newspaper was printed and that meant things going wrong and telephones ringing with news ten minutes late. She'd learned long ago that he was different on a Friday. You didn't ask favors of him then or expect him to listen to what your worst friend had said on the school bus. You waited for Saturday when the newspaper would be out and his day of tension would be over.

Her eyes wandered from the window, thinking of her father. Then she heard a movement or perhaps just felt it

and looked back to the window and he was there. Her first thought was amazement that he could be there on a Friday. Then the relief came in and she smiled and didn't want to say anything. Looking was enough.

John Fleming pressed near the window, hating the glass which separated them. He said, "How are you now?" Which was a silly question. Then he said, "Your mother will be here this afternoon. I just came this morning on the off-chance."

Gail wanted to ask, what time is it? But after a moment it didn't seem to matter. Then she asked, "What day is it?"

It was the first time she had spoken coherently since that afternoon in the stream. Her father leaned closer, his breath smudging the glass. He could not understand what she said so he talked quickly, in the hope that one of the disjointed sentences would be an answer.

"We've been here every afternoon—Mummy as well as me—except on Fridays, when only Mummy comes. You know what Fridays are."

So it isn't Friday, Gail thought.

"And Dr. Craig is very pleased—not as serious as it might have been—they know a lot about it now."

About what, Gail thought? Simultaneously she tried to move her legs.

"And everyone at school, they've been asking. They're sending flowers as soon as you're well enough. And your form teacher—Mr. Scott—he's going to write. And last Sunday the Curate—he said prayers in the Mission Church."

For me, Gail thought? Everyone praying for me? She imagined all the heads bowed in prayer and for a moment she was pleased because she'd not had so much attention before. Then her imagination looked beyond the congregation to the choir, where one of the senior choir boys had his eyes open. Rod Jennings, Gail thought. I bet he didn't. He wouldn't pray for Windy Fleming.

As she decided this she tried again to move her legs. Her right leg moved a little. The movement told her how hard the bed was; not like her bed at home, which was the best bed in the world. Then she tried to move her left leg, but her left leg would not move. She tried again while her father said, "Everyone keeps asking. We all miss you, even Rod Jennings. Even he says it's not the same."

Gail didn't hear. She was thinking about her left leg. She tried again and the pain in her back was searing. She didn't realize that she had screamed until she saw her father's distress and realized there were nurses in the room. A sister pulled the curtains abruptly, shutting her father out. Then hands were moving her in the bed, voices were talking to her, but all she could do was scream because now she knew what had happened to her leg.

"Stop that noise."

The voice was sharp and she realized that Dr. Craig was there. There was a moment of shock, for he had not spoken to her like that before.

"It's confined to your left leg. It might have been both."

Gail didn't want to hear. The only thought in her head was I know what it is, I've heard about it. You never walk again.

"Look." Dr. Craig gestured and two nurses turned back the covers expertly. "I'll show you."

Gail looked at her legs, astonished that the left appeared no different from the right. That was surely wrong. It should have been withered and ugly. It should have showed something.

"I touch your right foot. Look." The doctor touched

her right foot. "And your toes move. I tap your right knee. Look. And your lower leg moves."

It did, too. Gail was delighted.

"But I touch your left foot . . ."

Gail saw his hand on her left foot. She felt nothing.

"I even tickle your left foot. Look."

Gail watched. She wanted to say, I used to be able to spread my toes. Wider than Rod Jennings ever could.

"No response," Dr. Craig said. "Then your left knee and still there's nothing."

Gail looked away.

"But it's confined to your left leg and you must be grateful for that. Prompt attention, the skill of your family doctor in making a quick diagnosis, and the experience we have gained in recent years. You must be grateful for all that."

Still Gail looked away. She watched the curtains where her father had been. She wanted to say, why me? Why did it have to happen to me?

"I want to see you trying to do all I ask. Do you understand?"

He waited a long time and finally Gail pretended to agree.

"Because if you try, and if all the resources we have here are concentrated on you, there's a good chance you'll be among the lucky."

Lucky? Gail bit her lip. Can it be lucky to have one leg paralyzed? She saw what would happen when at last she got out of here and went back to the world where everyone ran and played and where the greatest honor was to be in the school team. For a while other children, even older children, prefects even, would be curious about her leg. But within a month they wouldn't care. They would run and leave her. Especially Rod Jennings. He would look down his nose at the girl who was not only a girl, which was bad enough, but a girl who had one leg in a steel cage.

"You and me." Dr. Craig's voice was kind again, making it a promise. "We'll do it together."

He stood back a pace as the nurses replaced the covers and tucked them in. He was waiting for Gail to look at him and after a while she did. Her eyes were hot with hatred because her imagination could hear other girls running and in a way it seemed to be his fault.

"There's nothing to be afraid of," Dr. Craig said. "Not if you make up your mind."

CHAPTER THREE

Adults and children joined a conspiracy to prove that there was nothing to be afraid of. There were letters, flowers, chocolates, get-well cards. Once even Rod Jennings came with his mother.

Mrs. Jennings said at the window, "Hullo, Gail." Then she nudged her son and Rod said, "Hi, Windy." Mrs. Jennings shot him a glare because nicknames were not nice; especially now with the poor little girl a cripple.

But Gail answered, "Hi, Flannel-ears," and for a second she and Rod shared a smile which Mrs. Jennings did not understand.

"He misses you," Mrs. Jennings said. "Never mind what he says. We all hope you'll be home soon."

That was the trouble; all the visitors either mentioned home or reminded her of it and she dared not dream of home. She was like a homesick sailor in a foreign land. She knew she could not go and the bleakest minutes of each day were when the people at the window moved away.

Her father and mother were always the first to come and the last to leave. They did not talk much, for the glass made conversation a strain. But the assurance that they were there was comforting, like having money in the bank. She could understand why a miser needed to look at his money. She needed to look at her parents in the same way.

"Did Mrs. Jennings tell you?" her mother said. "Their cat has had kittens."

Gail knew she was meant to show incredulity. So she widened her eyes like incredulity.

"Yes, again," Mrs. Fleming said. "Four of them, one ginger. She's trying to find homes."

But Mrs. Jennings wouldn't, Gail thought, because none of the moorland cottages wanted cats. There were already too many. She-cats were the best hunters of mice and rats, but many of the moorland cottages would not have a she-cat because of this recurring problem of what to do with the kittens.

Then there was silence for a while, giving Gail time to be sad about Mrs. Jennings' kittens.

After a while her father said, "I had a puncture going home yesterday. That back wheel."

Gail imagined him getting out and taking off his coat and fretting because he was no use with tools. Give him a typewriter and his tobacco-stained fingers were nimble. But give him jack or brace or screwdriver and he fumbled and puffed and blamed the tools; becoming a mildly comic figure who could not see the joke until the emergency was over. Not until then could he laugh at himself.

Gail smiled, imagining how long the wheel change had taken. He answered the smile as he said, "You know what I'm like."

That moment when they shared a smile was absolutely private, as though they were alone in the world. John Fleming felt it and was guilty about it. He reached for the mother's arm, bringing Mrs. Fleming into the private moment.

"You know how I need your mother to get me out of a mess."

Gail looked at her mother, sensing that her mother didn't really approve the joke which her father's clumsiness had become. Mrs. Fleming wanted him to be clever with machines, useful with power drills like Mr. Jennings.

Well, he's not Mr. Jennings, Gail thought. My father's clever, different. My father's special. She meant the thought to be only in her head but it showed in her eyes and Mrs. Fleming saw it and was baffled.

The bafflement showed in the way she removed her arm and changed the subject and when she was talking, it seemed that her father was the one left out. Gail looked at him to see if he had noticed but his eyes showed nothing.

"They're bringing you in television," Mrs. Fleming said. "I talked about it with Dr. Craig. He agreed as long as you don't watch too long and tire yourself."

For a while television was important. It ate the hours of early evening so that they were not as slow as chewing gum. But television was only in the evenings. She needed diversion during the day. When she was strong enough to sit up for short periods, Dr. Craig allowed her mother to bring books, her father to bring sketching pad and paints and exercise books.

The gifts emphasized the difference between her parents. Her mother wanted her to widen her knowledge so that when at last she returned to school, she would not be backward. But her father understood that she needed also to make her own world; to exercise her imagination by scribbling and painting. Her writing always became scribbling because her thoughts were always galloping, miles ahead of her right hand. Her pen could never catch up.

At first she wrote elaborate stories about a girl and a boy who shared fantastic adventures; the girl always rescuing the boy at the eleventh hour to prove her charity, the boy never expressing gratitude, proving that heroines are not appreciated in their own lifetime. But slowly the saga of adventures on the moor—including secret caves and quicksand and castles that vanished in the night— changed from fantasies to the expression of her most cherished dream. Each day the names of the boy and girl changed. So did the details of what happened. But the horse never did.

The horse was always a wonder horse, winning the Derby one day, the Grand National the next. The paintings became illustrations for the stories, and in the center of each illustration stood the horse. Sometimes it stood alone, with the wind in its mane and tail. Sometimes there was a girl at its head in proof of ownership. Occasionally she added a boy because you had to be fair. But always the horse was big and proud, as high on the hill as a king.

It began as a black horse and when the black panel of her paint box was empty it became brown; after that a chestnut. When the plausible colors were gone, it became green. It didn't matter that no horse could ever be green.

Dr. Craig was mildly interested in her stories, glancing at the adventure stories and smiling at the castle which vanished in the night. But his interest tightened as the stories grew out of fantasy to the expression of her dream. He read them carefully and admired the illustrations, even when the horse turned green.

Finally he said, "Is that what you want?"

"Yes," Gail said, knowing she would never have it. Then she remembered Topper and looked away.

"I always wanted a horse." Dr. Craig smiled. "When I

was your age, they told me to wait until I could afford it. And now I can afford it, they say I'm too old and stiff."

Every morning, when he examined her and the nurses moved her in the bed, they talked about the story which she would write today. Soon she was telling him about Topper, confiding more than she had ever confided to anyone, except her father. It seemed that Dr. Craig became very like her father, and at the same time it seemed that she became his favorite patient, as special to him as previously she had been special only to her father.

They shared secrets; she telling him every detail of the horse she would never have, he telling her of a film he had seen many years ago. The film had been *Wings of the Morning*, and he could remember little of it except that there had been gypsies and a horse. A beautiful horse. The beauty of that horse had seized his young imagination and had become a memory that tugged with longing. Gail knew Dr. Craig would never forget it; any more than she would ever forget the horse which existed only in her imagination.

"You're doing very well," Dr. Craig said. "Not bored now?"

"No," Gail said, and that was true. She was as busy with her stories and illustrations as she would have been at school with French and algebra.

"Not thinking only of getting out?"

He did not say "Not thinking only of going home" and that made it easier for Gail to answer.

"No," she said, and that was also true. It seemed now that she belonged to this world of nurses and doctors, of seven o'clock sponging and three o'clock tea.

"Right then." The doctor's voice changed. "We can start the real business of getting you well."

Well? Gail thought. I'm well already. I can sit up, no

headaches hardly ever, and I can write and paint. I feel fine.

"Really well," Dr. Craig emphasized. "You're strong enough to take it."

She didn't understand what he meant until he made her attempt small exercises; first her right leg, which was easy, then her left, which seemed impossible. The pains came back. They were worse than she had thought any pain could be; her leg and back, her neck and head.

Half-past ten each morning. That was the time it began. No sitting up now, no writing pads or exercise books. Only Dr. Craig, insisting, coaxing, teasing, bullying; compelling her to attempt what she knew she could not.

"You've made up your mind," Dr. Craig snapped. "You're giving in to it."

All right, Gail thought, I'm giving in. She glared at him, her eyes hot with hatred. She couldn't believe that this was the man who had seemed so like her father.

She said, "My father wouldn't hurt me."

His manner changed then. He sat on the bed and tried to explain. She mustn't resist him, hate him. She must trust him to guide her through the pain to what was on the other side.

"You'll be able to walk again, perhaps even run again. I promise you. But first you've got to make those muscles do what you want."

He knew that truly she did not want it. She didn't want to be a cripple, but most of all she didn't want to wake up every morning to more exercises and the certainty of pain. To be left alone was better. Her books and paints and paper could be made to seem enough.

She said, "If you'll only leave me alone."

Dr. Craig stood up. There was sadness in his slowness,

and the sadness deceived her. She supposed he was giving up and that she had won.

But in the morning he was back. Grimly he insisted and she had to obey. She hated to see the door open and the nurses hurrying; to know that he was coming. She made whimpering cries before the pain began, then screamed when it did.

"You're getting better." Dr. Craig's voice was urgent. "This is the first stage and you're getting through it."

These sessions left her weak and tired, but she would not close her eyes. She watched the window, not daring to close her eyes until she was sure that her father was there. Not until then did she let sleep come in, trusting her father to protect her.

John Fleming stayed at the window, his collar turned up and his hatbrim turned down because the rain was heavy. But Mrs. Fleming was not with him. She was in a consulting room, talking with Dr. Craig, her distress unable to understand what the doctor was trying to say.

"Gail's worse," Mrs. Fleming said. "Every afternoon so exhausted."

Dr. Craig began to say, "She's getting through it," but the mother interrupted.

"Can't she come home?"

Dr. Craig shook his head.

"But there's no danger of infection now. And surely I can do whatever needs to be done."

The doctor's glance sharpened. "What do you think needs to be done?"

"Well, look after her. Comfort her."

"No."

"But surely . . ." Mrs. Fleming said.

Dr. Craig chose his words carefully. "If you do that, Mrs. Fleming, she'll never fight her way through." He saw what she was going to say. His voice quickened as he interrupted. "It's not comforting she needs or being made a fuss of. It's determination. Courage. Making her do what she knows will be very painful."

Mrs. Fleming forgot what she had been going to say. She began to think about it.

"It's not easy to watch," Dr. Craig said. "I don't think either you or Mr. Fleming could watch it for long."

Mrs. Fleming thought about that, too. She stared at a calendar, as though the red dates were important. After a while she said, "It's not fair to make a child endure it."

"There's no other way."

"But she's not used to it." Mrs. Fleming flashed a glance. "She's always been a coward about pain."

"We all are," Dr. Craig said.

Again Mrs. Fleming waited a long time. Then she said, "If you're sure there's no other way."

"There isn't," Dr. Craig said. "At present she's struggling against it and hating me, but she's making progress."

Mrs. Fleming's glance wondered if he was telling the truth. "But if only I could touch her, put my arms round her. If only my husband and I weren't kept from her by that window."

Dr. Craig nodded, understanding resentment of the glass between. Quietly he said, "I promise you this. As soon as Gail can stand, walk a little, as soon as she's on the way to complete recovery, then she can come home."

Mrs. Fleming watched his face, seeking a sign that this was a genuine promise.

"I promise," Dr. Craig said. "If I can get her through the next few days, she'll be able to try standing."

The way he said "standing" made it a milestone on a long journey. Mrs. Fleming noticed the strain in his face.

It flashed through her mind that perhaps he had children of his own; that perhaps all his life was not in this hospital, dedicated to the service of others.

She asked, "Have you any children?"

Dr. Craig shook his head. Sadness darkened his eyes and the sadness stopped her from enquiring further. She turned away as she said, "Thank you, Doctor. I've some idea of all you've done and I'm very grateful."

Dr. Craig accompanied her to the door. He opened it for her, then held it until she looked at him. His smile was rueful as he said, "Perhaps . . . sometime . . . your daughter will be grateful, too."

But Gail did not understand that she had anything to be grateful for. She opened her eyes, sensing a movement at the window, afraid that her father was about to leave. But the movement was her mother, coming from the consulting room to join her father.

Gail saw the look which her parents shared; her father's glance of hope, then her mother's slight head shake. Gail had learned to read this language of signs which her parents sometimes used. She knew that the head shake was in some way about her.

She waited until they were looking at her; until they could read her lips if they could not hear. Then she said, "Let me come home. Why can't I come home?"

CHAPTER FOUR

Going home became the only idea in Gail's head. She did not write stories or paint illustrations; she did not read or attempt the work which the form teacher sent. She lay on a side and stared at nothing, yearning for the place where her parents were; for the room with sloping beams and a narrow window, where Quakers had met two hundred years ago.

Her father had told her about the room when he'd bought the house. Quakers in the eighteenth century had been mocked and oppressed. They had needed places where they could meet in secret, and the house called Gorse Blossom had been one of them. They had come across the wild moor to the back door; sure of a welcome, of food and shelter. Then they had climbed to the upper room and had sat in peace, waiting for the words of God to inspire them.

From the first she'd been fascinated by the room. Sometimes she imagined strange people coming in. They wore black and the men kept on their hats. They were grave and silent but their silence was not threatening. Most of the men looked like Gary Cooper, because she'd seen an old film in which Gary Cooper had played a Quaker in America.

Mrs. Fleming, guessing what was going on in her head, had been afraid that the room would frighten her. But nothing in this room could frighten her. She felt safe there. It had her bookcase and homework desk. It had those dolls cots which she seldom played with now but would not give away. Behind the door was the one rosette which she had won riding Topper. It was the only room in the world which she had helped to make.

She saw the room so clearly that sometimes it seemed she was there, that this hospital ward was just a dream from which she'd soon awaken. She began to build fantasies around her need to return; devising plans to get away without the hospital being aware until it was too late. She would creep from the ward at night and thumb a lift and pretend to be sleepwalking when the driver was bewildered by a girl in a nightdress. She would outwit them all; the nurses and doctors, especially Dr. Craig. Even her parents, for in these fantasies it seemed that even her parents did not want her to come home.

"You can go home," Dr. Craig said.

Her astonishment became suspicion. She knew the hospital would not give her up so easily.

"As soon as you can walk to that wall."

He pointed. The wall was about three yards from the bed. It seemed a long way.

"Not hopping," Dr. Craig emphasized. "Or being helped. But absolutely on your own. With your left leg doing some of it."

She looked at the wall. She knew she could not do it.

"You can," Dr. Craig said. "You will. Provided you really fight."

Gail fought. She tried to stand alone, depending on her right leg to be enough. But even that was more than she could manage. Dizziness sang in her ears. She would have fallen if a nurse's arm had not guided her down to the bed.

"It'll be easier tomorrow," Dr. Craig said.

Now Gail was not afraid of tomorrow. She was impatient for it, eager to try again because every attempt must earn her the right to go home. She wasn't afraid of pain or of the humiliation of falling. If she fell, she would get up. And if others tried to help, she would shake off their help and get up alone. That would show Dr. Craig.

The need to show Dr. Craig became a part of her determination. She stood beside the bed, fighting the sea sound in her ears, her face pale and tense. The nurses dropped their hands. For a moment she swayed and the sea sound drowned her senses. Then she straightened. They could see her determination. She moved her right leg in a shuffle. She tried to move her left.

Her left leg could do nothing. It would not follow. It was stupid. She cried out in despair, because what could you do with a stupid leg? Then the nurses were there and suddenly she was back in the bed and Dr. Craig was bending over her.

"Very good. Keep fighting like that and every day will be a day nearer home."

They kept saying "home" and she kept trying. It was a private fight which her parents never saw. They saw only what it did to her; leaving her so exhausted that some afternoons she was asleep long before they came to the window. They could not know that now her tiredness was different. There was no despair in it or resentment. Only impatience because tomorrow was so far off and not until tomorrow could she try again.

Finally she walked. She moved a little; only a little

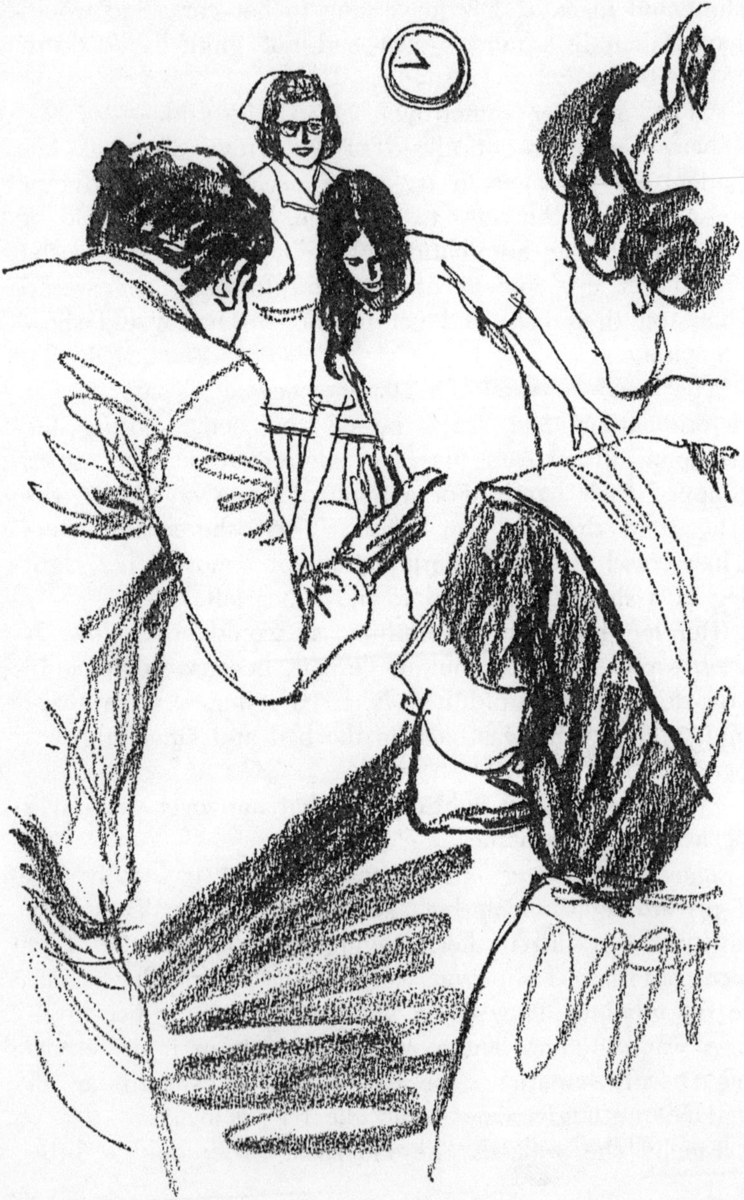

but enough to have the nurses excited and Dr. Craig smiling congratulations. The movement ended in a fall, but falling did not matter. She forgot it in the excitement of small success. She was panting and laughing as the nurses stooped for her and lifted her to the bed.

"They've got a nerve to call you Windy," Dr. Craig said.

There was no hostility between them after that. All her trust came back. The hand which he held out each morning, tempting her to reach it, became the hand of her father; calling her toward home and the room with the sloping ceiling and the view of the moor from the window.

The feeling in the ward changed. No longer a white prison, it became a stage with a performance every morning when she showed off for the nurses, for all the doctors who came to see. But most of all she showed off for Dr. Craig, laughing as she reached for his hand, her eyes shining as she grasped it.

There was jubilation in the ward, making it a place of triumph. Everyone seemed to be smiling, and when her parents came to the window they were smiling too. Nurses were talking openly of home; mentioning next week although only Dr. Craig could decide and there might be a setback.

There was no setback. Gail reached her wall four mornings out of five. Then her impatience to get home was like her ache years ago for Christmas Day; waiting so long that it seemed the day would never come. That's why she couldn't believe it when Dr. Craig said, "Tomorrow."

It sounded too good to be true. "Truly?" she said.

"Truly." Dr. Craig straightened from the bed. "You'll be home tomorrow."

He moved to the bottom of the bed yet he did not leave. He stayed there, looking at her.

"Well, Windy, we did it."

She answered his smile, making him the most important man in the world except her father. The silence in the ward had a strange sadness, as though they had shared something which was ending. She did not want to admit that tomorrow or the next day there would be somebody else in this bed; that he would be coming in to somebody else.

"Not so bad was it?"

She guessed he was remembering her hatred. She felt ashamed. "No," she said.

"And once a month I'll come and see you."

That was a surprise. Her face showed how pleased she was.

"Just to see how you're getting on." Dr. Craig began to move away. "Good-night, Windy."

Every evening he'd said good-night as he went out, but this was different. This was more than a good-night. It was as final as good-bye. She watched the door through which he had passed, and for a moment her sadness was such that almost she did not want to leave.

But there was no sadness when she awoke in the morning. The nurses came bustling, making the morning different, important. The only thought in her head was when. How soon?

"Eleven o'clock," the sister said. "The ambulance will be here then."

The hours from seven o'clock to eleven became the slowest ever invented. Gail watched a nurse pack the articles which she could take; but that was soon done for the articles were few. She could not take books and sketch pads and illustrations.

"It's the rule," the sister said. "Every precaution must be taken."

They carried away her books, her stories and illustrations. Gail guessed that somewhere in the basement someone would burn them. There was a stab of resentment as she imagined her stories shriveling in the flames, and in that instant she realized that she had ceased to be a favorite patient. She'd become just another patient going out. It seemed the hospital had more important people to look after.

All right, Gail thought, if that's how you want it. She stared at the window, looking out to the real world where her home was.

Home seemed very near when her father appeared. He came to the window, half an hour early but still hurrying. His breath smudged the glass as he said, "They're letting me come in the ambulance with you."

Nurses lifted her to a wheel chair and a porter came to push it. But they did not take her from the ward. They were waiting for someone, glancing at their watches, then at the corridor. Dr. Craig came a minute late. He hurried in, his white coat flapping. He gave her a brief glance, then nodded to a nurse.

"Make sure she travels warm. She's been in here a long time."

Gail watched his face for a sign that they had shared something special which they would always remember. But this was not the Dr. Craig of yesterday. He did not meet her eyes. His "Good-bye, Gail" was formal. It couldn't care less.

The porter wheeled her to the corridor and along it to the lift. The nurse walked beside her, then stood beside her as the lift sank. The gate slid back. She was wheeled out to the tiled passage, toward the opened doors.

There was sunshine and the song of birds. Flowers were nodding in the gardens. She looked up to the sky and thought, it's over. It was like coming out of prison.

Her father was waiting near the ambulance. She reached out a hand, reaching for him as she had reached for that other hand during morning exercises. He took it and they held hands for as long as the ambulance men would allow.

Then one said, "If you don't mind, sir," and John Fleming stood back, watching as the men wheeled the chair up the ramp. The nurse helped them transfer her from the chair to a bed. The porter took away the chair and her father came up the ramp and sat near her. Doors closed. The engine awoke. The ambulance moved. Gail could not see but she imagined the ambulance going down the drive while the hospital windows receded like leaves taken away by a stream. She thought, I'll never go back there again. Already it seemed a dreadful place.

Her father did not speak until the ambulance had passed out of the city and was traveling steadily along a good road. Then he said, "Be on the moor soon."

She knew when they were near the moor because the driver changed gears and the engine growled at the long climb. They were climbing out of the valley to the hill where the moor began.

"This is it," her father said.

She knew every bend, every rise and fall. They were passing the big tor on the right; the granite rocks like a ruined castle and haunted by black hounds when the moon was bright. It was the scene of many of her stories. She was as fascinated by it as she was frightened.

On the left was the Berry Brook, meandering down the hill and grumbling to itself like an old man trying to find his pension. Soon they would pass the hawthorn tree, the only tree to survive the wind on this face of the moor. It had been leaning ever since she could remember; always threatening to fall but never falling, like one of those old soldiers who are wounded often but who never die.

She waited until they had passed the hawthorn. Then she waited for the rise and imagined the farmhouse on the right; the house and shippens built of granite because that was the only stone on the moor. There would be black cattle in the walled-in fields and somewhere near the house there would be geese, their necks as long as periscopes, their heads high in suspicion when they heard the ambulance. She knew why the farmer kept geese. They made good sentries. None could approach the lonely farm without the geese sounding the alarm. The sound they made was as loud as barking.

A mile away was the house with evil windows. They were gabled windows and the gables were like eyebrows, making the stare of the windows as black as dark glasses. She used this house in some of her stories. It was the place where robbers plotted, where blood dripped through the ceiling every night.

On the other side of the house was a high hill and beyond the hill were miles of heather stretching to Princetown. The name made her shiver, for Princetown was the prison; gray and forbidding, the most formidable in Britain. She'd seen it only once. After that she'd closed her eyes when the family car went through the town.

They came to the bridge, built long ago when there had been pack horses on the moor. A bridge wide enough for a horse with panniers on each side; that had been all the builders had thought would ever be necessary. None had imagined lorries and coaches. The ambulance had only inches to spare as it crept up one side and down the other.

After the bridge came the last hill and the driver changed gear for it. Slowly the ambulance climbed and when it reached the top, Gail knew what the driver could see. A wilderness, stretching to the sky; heather and bracken and granite, with nothing moving unless the wind decided.

The long road seemed to go on toward the horizon, as pale and distinct as a scar across your forehead. Gail hoped the driver knew where the fork was. Strangers often missed it, for the narrow track which branched to the left had no signpost. You had to know that two miles along it was one of the oldest hamlets on the moor.

The hamlet was Gorse Blossom, first mentioned in 1360. She'd learned that from her father. Gorse Blossom had been a small farm, cut out of the wilderness by early pioneers, then improved by generations until by the nineteenth century it had become one of the most important farms on the moor. It had been big enough to employ farm hands and those hands had needed cottages. So granite cottages had been built nearby, giving Gorse Blossom a new importance on the map.

Until the second world war families had continued to farm it in the traditional way; grazing cattle, sheep, and ponies on the hills and tilling enough to supply their needs. Then, in 1948, the twentieth century had found isolated Gorse Blossom and had touched it with a wand of many changes.

Its cultivated land had been sold; its rights of common grazing had been transferred to a bigger farm on the other side of the hill. A wealthy businessman, rich enough to afford a weekend house, had bought the house and improved it; introducing mains water, electricity, bathroom and modern kitchen. Then he had tired of it and gone to the Bahamas and the house had changed hands frequently until 1959, when her father had bought it.

Meanwhile the cottages nearby had been improved by a series of owners. Some were retired people, who had no children and who lived on Service pensions. Others were foresters, who worked in the plantations on the other side of the hill. Mr. Jennings was one of them and his son Rod was the only other child at Gorse Blossom.

He won't be home, Gail thought. Rod'll be at school, driving his teachers up the wall. She was glad Rod would not be there to see her carried from the ambulance. He'd only look down his nose at her helplessness and make it further proof of what he'd always said. Girls should never be allowed.

The ambulance followed the fork toward Gorse Blossom and Gail hugged herself; imagining the house getting bigger, imagining the window of her bedroom looking out. Her mother would be coming to the porch, then down the slope to the gate. Now she would be opening the gate, holding it back as the ambulance approached. Gail imagined the wind in her mother's hair; a sunshine wind which did no more than ruffle one side, making it a chestnut haze. Gail liked her mother's hair best when it was ruffled in this way. She imagined her mother holding up a hand to it.

The ambulance moved up the slope to the porch and her mother's voice was calling, impatient for the doors to open. John Fleming stood up, half-crouching because he was so tall. He shared that impatience for the doors to open.

An ambulance man opened the doors. Gail saw her mother, the porch, the windows. There was a minute of excited confusion. Then the men helped the nurse to transfer her to a stretcher. She was lifted out and down. Again she felt that curious sensation, like a magic carpet with only the sky to look at.

"In here," Mrs. Fleming said.

They carried her through the porch to the hall, then up the stairs with the stretcher leaning like a seasick deck. The door of the Quakers' room was open; her bed was waiting. She saw at once that the eiderdown was new. When the nurse moved the eiderdown, she saw that the blankets were pale green instead of blue.

The room was too small for all the people in it. There was more confusion before the ambulance men went out. Her father led them down the stairs. Over his shoulder he was thanking them, offering coffee or tea. Or bottles of beer if they preferred. The men murmured no thanks, they had to get back. The murmur of their voices faded.

The nurse gave Mrs. Fleming an envelope. "From Dr. Craig. He said be sure to follow it precisely."

"Of course," Mrs. Fleming answered. But she did not open it. She stuffed it into a pocket and waited for the nurse to leave; for the hospital finally to admit that it no longer owned her daughter. Gail was surprised by her mother's stiffness, coldness. It seemed that she resented the nurse's air of authority.

"I was also told to tell you . . ." The nurse hesitated, sensing the coldness. "Should you be alarmed at any time, please ring Dr. Craig at once."

"All right," Mrs. Fleming said.

Then the nurse was going down the stairs to the hall, where Mr. Fleming waited to show her out. The doors of the ambulance closed. Its engine made striving sounds. Mrs. Fleming listened to the sounds receding. Then she turned to her daughter and crouched beside the bed, touching Gail for the first time. It seemed that her touch was saying more than words could say.

Gail looked around the room, trying to believe that less than two hours ago she had been far away. The ceiling, the beams, the wallpaper, the window. The television set in a corner, that was new. It had a fourteen-inch screen.

"Mr. Jennings fixed it for us," Mrs. Fleming said. "He knew what a help it would be."

Gail's glance moved to a loud-speaker on the homework desk. She guessed it was connected to television or radio, but Mrs. Fleming shook her head.

"Mr. Jennings fixed that, too. It was his idea. Listen."

Gail wondered what she was supposed to hear. There was a long pause. Then her father said, "Hullo, Gail." The voice was loud. It seemed that he was in the room.

"It's linked with the living room," Mrs. Fleming said. "You'll be able to hear voices down there. You'll never feel alone."

Gail began to realize that while she had been weaving fantasies, in which even her parents did not want her home, they had been preparing to help in any way they could. Her slight smile had shame in it. She looked to the bookshelves. The book jackets seemed the same, but she knew they were different.

"We had to change them," Mrs. Fleming said. "The health officer destroyed every copy in case of germs between the pages. But your father spent hours, days, weeks, looking for the same titles."

Gail moved her head enough to see her father coming in. Again they shared a secret moment and again for that moment the mother was left out.

"If there's anything," Mrs. Fleming said. "Anything you want, anything I can do."

There was a pleading in her voice, as though she knew she was being left out and did not want to be.

Gail moved her head, showing there was nothing. She was home. There seemed nothing else that she could ever want.

CHAPTER FIVE

Her first visitor was Rod. He came up the stairs with a bag of grapes in one hand and his geometry book in a pocket. Mrs. Jennings had given the grapes, cautioning him against eating any on the way and begging him to be "the little gentleman. Wipe your shoes when you go in and take that frown off. You're supposed to be sympathetic." The geometry book had been his idea.

Mrs. Fleming opened the door of the Quakers' room. She said, "Look who's come to see you." As though Gail needed to look. She'd known who it was as soon as she'd heard the stumping on the stairs. Nobody else ever stumped like that.

Then Rod came in, blushing a little because Mrs. Fleming was watching and might report his behavior to Mrs. Jennings. You could never tell with mothers.

"Hullo, Windy, they said you were home."

Gail wore her grand manner. "Hullo, Roderick, how nice of you to come." She might have been Elizabeth Barrett receiving a visitor to the invalid's couch at Wimpole Street.

Rod came near the bed. He held out the bag; not because he wanted her to have them but because any boy would feel a nit carrying grapes.

45

"Oh, thank you."

Gail didn't open the bag; partly because ladies didn't grab and partly because she could bet that Rod wanted half. "It's very kind," she said.

Mrs. Fleming smiled on their meeting. She thought it was charming. "Well, I'll leave you two. You must have such a lot to talk about and there's Daddy's meal in the oven."

She went out, leaving the two of them. They looked at each other. Gail noticed his crumpled blazer, ruined prematurely by being used as a goal post; he noticed the ribbon in her hair, the fancy frill of her bed jacket. Done up like a dog's dinner, he thought.

He almost said it, showing what he thought of her grand manner. Then he remembered that those in need of help can't be too critical and he needed help all right. He pulled the exercise book from his pocket.

It was folded as though school books didn't matter. She made an exclamation of disgust, imitating Mr. Scott who was the form teacher and took a dim view of such things. She would never abuse a book like that. Her father had taught her to respect books; especially exercise books which had wonderfully white pages for your stories to grow in.

"Geometry," Rod said.

She had already guessed. The day was Thursday and Thursday evening was always bad because its homework included geometry; as though French and Hereward the Wake weren't enough.

"Square on the hypoto and all that load."

Rod held out the book and she took it. Then he lost interest, trusting her to save him. He turned toward the bookshelves, looking at the titles. *Birds of Britain, Black Beauty, Treasure Island.* Not a Wild West among them.

Gail flipped the pages, glancing at the marks he had received in her absence. The marks were in red ink. So were the comments. "See me" was a favorite. The third time it had two exclamation marks to show that this was serious. Primly she asked, "How on earth did you manage while I was away?"

She knew, of course. The marks and comments were evidence; while the blots and scratching-out showed how desperate he had become. But she wanted him to admit that he had missed her.

"I didn't." Rod was still looking for *Billy the Kid* among the titles. "Every morning it was chronic."

She was delighted, for that should have shown him the importance of girls. They might not be able to catch a fish with their hands or bowl googlies or even shove in the second row; but they didn't have "See me" in their homework books. Neither were they frightened silly by Shakespeare and the Gulf Stream.

"This is easy enough." She looked at the untidy sketch which he had drawn. "It's Pythagoras."

Rod made a sound to show what he thought of Pythagoras. The Greek mathematician was in the same league as Macbeth and Attila and all that junk.

"It means the square on the hypotenuse is equal to the sum of the squares on the other two sides."

Rod made another sound. He seemed to be in pain.

"You've got to learn it," Gail said. "Otherwise you'll never take your General Certificate of Education."

"Hah," Rod said.

"It's not that easy, so you might as well show some interest."

He turned from the bookshelves and came back to the bed, watching as she worked it out. She used a page of notepaper, trusting him to copy it accurately when he got home. The problem was more difficult than she had pretended. She had to bite her pencil and concentrate, and when he was sure she was concentrating he opened the bag and pinched a grape.

Mrs. Fleming found him sitting on the floor while Gail frowned in concentration. She switched on the bedside lamp and moved to draw the curtains. The room became a private world, as warm and colorful as the secret world you sometimes see in the middle of a fire. Mrs. Fleming smiled on them, glad that Rod knew where to come for help and proud that Gail could give it.

"As long as you don't tire yourself," Mrs. Fleming said.

Gail decided to be tired, for the problem proved more difficult every minute and the only answer she could get might mean "See me" in the morning. If that happened, she could plead tiredness as an excuse. She wrote an answer and Rod asked no questions. He took the page and held up the bag. They ate grapes and did tricks with the pips until there were sounds of a hurrying car and her father was home.

Other friends came at the weekend. Betsy Brown was one. She played left-inner in the hockey team and had averaged A-minus at the end of last term. Liz Reynolds was another. She wanted to be a model and liked cutting fashion photographs from magazines.

Mrs. Fleming made them very welcome, trusting them to keep Gail in touch with school events. She was determined that Gail should be amused and diverted; never lost in the rut of boredom as she must have been in the hospital. Mrs. Fleming liked to hear giggling in the bedroom. She thought the giggling, the merriment, the feeling of young people in the house, were more important than Dr. Craig's list of what to do and when and for how long. She preferred to make her own routine.

The routine began at half-past seven, when Gail awakened. Her father talked with her as he shaved; keeping the doors of bedroom and bathroom opened, so that she could see him at the shaving mirror. She liked to hear about today; where he would go and the people he would meet. Sometimes he had to report a harvest-home or carnival or parish council meeting. Sometimes he had to interview people who were complaining; about high rates or increased rents or the desecration of graveyards by hooligans. Every day was different. Except Friday. Fridays were always the same. Then he had to stay in the office and watch the newspaper being made up; coping with late telephone calls and grumbling printers and sudden emergencies. He never talked much on Friday mornings. He always shaved hurriedly and cut himself and said, "This is a fine way to start the day." At half-past eight he left to be at his office by nine.

Mrs. Fleming brought up warm water, sponge and towel, bathing Gail's face and arms and hands. Then she brushed her hair, taking a long time over it and asking about the books Gail was reading. She was interested in "good" books, especially school books. She didn't often ask about the stories Gail was writing.

Shortly after nine Gail had breakfast; egg and bacon and mushrooms. Then Mrs. Fleming went away to wash the dishes and to tidy the kitchen, the bathroom and big bedroom. When she came back it was time for exercises.

At first Gail accepted them as a continuation of hospital routine, but she quickly saw that her mother took them less seriously than had the doctors and nurses. Mrs. Fleming held out a hand, calling her as Dr. Craig had done. But when Gail stopped halfway, losing confidence and afraid of falling, Mrs. Fleming did not wait. She came a stride to meet her and let halfway be enough.

"You're tired," she said. "You mustn't overdo it."

Then she helped Gail back to bed and tucked her in and made her comfortable; letting her have the rest of the morning for reading or writing, for painting the illustrations of her stories. In the afternoon she sat at the window and looked out to the moor. The colors of autumn were in the bracken; turning it pale brown like breakfast toast. The color of the gorse was yellow, like blobs of butter melting into the toast. She counted the sheep and wild ponies and watched an angler fishing for trout; never bored because there was so little to see but quiet in herself and contented. This was the moor as she had always known it and anywhere else was a foreign place.

She stayed at the window until a beetle showed on the moor; no larger than a beetle although if you waited long enough it grew bigger and bigger and became the school bus. The bus came down the hill and stopped. There were faces at the glass, hands waving from lowered windows. Gail waved in answer, recognizing the faces, even the hands. Meanwhile the door slid back and Rod got down.

His satchel was slung over a shoulder; bulging with books and plimsolls and woodwork apron. You might suppose him a very studious boy until you knew that half the books were *Pioneers of the Wild West* and *Racing Form* and *Gun Fight at the Lazy Y*. His cap was on the back of his head. His hair was fuzzed out in front. He mooched toward his house, not looking up to Gail's window while the girls in the bus were watching. Not until the bus had gone did he give a sign that he knew she was there. Sometimes the sign was couldn't-care-less. But on Thursdays he always waved, making her his best friend.

The school bus was one of the big events of Gail's day. The other was the return of her father.

It seemed to be a satisfactory routine until Dr. Craig came on the first of his monthly visits. Gail heard his car draw up; heard his voice in the hall, asking questions while her mother said, "She's doing very well. Not so tired as she used to be and always very patient."

Mrs. Fleming led the doctor up the stairs. Over a shoulder she said, "Of course we do everything possible to keep her amused. Friends come and visit. And there's a boy who lives nearby."

Gail glanced around the room, wanting Dr. Craig to notice her books, her curtains and carpet; wanting him to be impressed. Her eyes were on the door as the doctor came in. He wore a sheepskin coat, showing that the moor was cold to one accustomed to central heating. His gray eyes were crinkled in a smile.

"Hullo, Gail."

She was disappointed that he did not use her nickname. Perhaps he had forgotten it. Then he sat on the edge of the bed, looking at her closely.

"We're very pleased," Mrs. Fleming said. "Even her school work, she's keeping up with that. And having so many friends, that helps to keep her in touch."

Dr. Craig did not take his eyes from Gail. "Well, let's see how you're doing." He began to turn back the covers.

"Oh," Mrs. Fleming said, "she's done it once today."

He still turned back the covers. "She can do it again."

"But it makes her so tired. And she's so afraid of falling."

"She can do it twice. Can't you, Windy?"

Dr. Craig did not wait for Gail to answer. He slid an arm beneath her knees, lifted her legs from the bed and waited until her feet were on the carpet. Then he stood back, watching as she straightened and stood and prepared to move.

51

"Come to me." Mrs. Fleming held out a hand. "Show the doctor how well you can do."

Gail moved right foot, then left foot, leaning to touch her mother's hand. When her fingers missed, Mrs. Fleming moved nearer and caught her hand and said, "Well done." Over a shoulder she added, "She does this every morning. No pain at all."

Dr. Craig did not answer. He put an arm around Gail, guiding her to the bed and replacing the covers. She watched his face, knowing that his silence was wrong. There was disappointment in it. He didn't seem to be listening to what her mother said.

"Good-bye, Windy."

Gail answered, "Good-bye, Dr. Craig."

"I'll be coming again, of course."

It should have been a promise, but it seemed to be a threat. Gail saw the sharpness in his eyes, and realized how bitterly she had disappointed him. Then she strained to hear what they were saying on the stairs and in the hall. She heard him say, "There's one thing you ought to know."

At once the atmosphere of the house went cold with a sense of foreboding. Mrs. Fleming didn't want to hear. Gail imagined her stiff coldness, as resentful of the doctor as she had been of the nurse.

"Your daughter's made no progress at all."

"That's nonsense." Mrs. Fleming's protest was quick. "She's always cheerful. And every morning she does her best."

"Not enough. She's walking no better than a month ago."

"She does all she can."

"You must make her do more."

"I've no intention of hurting her."

"You must," Dr. Craig said.

Gail cringed beneath the covers. She thought her mother very brave to stand up to him when he spoke like that. None of the nurses in the hospital had ever dared. Neither had the younger doctors.

"You must always be demanding more. Because if you don't, your daughter will never walk alone."

Dr. Craig paused as though that were all. Gail imagined him turning away, picking up his hat from the small table in the hall. Then he said, "That list the nurse gave you. You must follow its instructions to the letter. Trying a little more each day because each day Gail ought to be that little stronger. Making her when she doesn't think she can."

Mrs. Fleming began to protest, but Dr. Craig interrupted. "You must promise, Mrs. Fleming."

She hesitated, then made a sound as though she was promising. Then they were saying good-byes and the doctor was leaving and when his car had gone, Mrs. Fleming came to the bedroom. Gail watched her face to see what was there. She saw that her mother would not force her, would not hurt her. She put her arms around her mother, leaning into the gentle comfort. She was crying, frightened by the doctor's disappointment, by the memory of what he had made her do in the hospital.

"It's all right," Mrs. Fleming said. "Don't be frightened. I won't let anyone hurt you."

John Fleming did not fully realize what was happening until another month passed and Dr. Craig came again. This time his face showed nothing as Gail stumbled toward her mother, almost falling into her mother's arms and crying there because she knew what her mother would not admit; that far from making progress, she could not walk as well as she had at the beginning.

Mrs. Fleming glared at the doctor above the girl's head. "It's you. She's frightened of you."

Dr. Craig didn't answer. He turned away as Mrs. Fleming said, "You can see what it does to her."

He waited while she helped Gail to the bed and made her comfortable. Then he said, "Mrs. Fleming, what's your husband's telephone number?"

"Why?"

"I want to talk to him."

Mrs. Fleming began to say, "My husband agrees with me. It's pointless tormenting her . . ."

But Dr. Craig interrupted. "It's serious, Mrs. Fleming. I'd like to fix an appointment for tomorrow."

There was urgency in the "tomorrow." It frightened Mrs. Fleming. "But why my husband? Why can't you tell me?"

"Because last time I was here you promised." He sounded sad rather than angry. "I don't need to ask whether you've carried it out. I can see you haven't."

"I'm not doing it." Mrs. Fleming's eyes were wild. "I'm not watching my child suffer."

"So I must see him."

His sadness was more frightening than anger would have been. Mrs. Fleming did not want to give the number of the newspaper, yet she dared not refuse. There was a defiant tilt to her head as she said, "You can phone from here."

"Thank you," Dr. Craig said.

Gail hugged the covers close to her chin as she listened to the sounds of dialing, then his request to speak to John Fleming. There was a pause while the switchboard girl put the call through to the editorial department. A swank name for a small, disheveled room which had two desks and three typewriters and crumpled papers in the waste basket.

Then her father was at the other end and Dr. Craig was suggesting an appointment; stressing the necessity when her father expressed surprise. At the hospital. Tomorrow. Three o'clock. Her father must have agreed, for Dr. Craig said, "Excellent, I'll see you then."

He put down the phone and the silence in the house became frightening. Gail felt the hostility. She imagined her mother's pale coldness.

"I'm sorry, Mrs. Fleming." Dr. Craig opened the front door and the hiss of rain was as loud as the hiss of a snake. "But it's essential that my instructions are carried out."

It sounded ruthless and again Gail cringed, making him an evil man who would not let her rest. She watched the landing, waiting for her mother to come up. Then she said, "Daddy won't let them hurt me. I know he won't."

Mrs. Fleming shook her head. No, of course he wouldn't. But Gail saw that she was thinking of something else. Her eyes were frightened.

It seemed that something easy and pleasant had ended; a happy period, when mother and daughter had come closer than at any time since babyhood. Another period was about to begin, dominated by Dr. Craig although he would not be there. Gail listened to the silence in the house. It seemed that suddenly the house had forgotten the way to laugh.

Even her father was different. He came back from his talk with Dr. Craig and his face was thin and haggard. His smile was a ghost as he sat on the stool beside her bed.

"I'm leaving for work later each day for a while. I've fixed it with the editor. He understands."

Gail wondered what the editor understood that she did not.

55

"I'm going to see you walk each morning. You must do more. Try harder. Because if you don't."

John Fleming hesitated, looking ahead to something in the future.

"Dr. Craig warned me." Again John Fleming hesitated. "He said if you don't, you might become a permanent invalid."

Gail didn't understand all that it might mean. She was less frightened by it than he was.

His smile quivered as he touched her hand. "I said you'd do anything for me."

Yet in the morning Gail could do no more for him than she had for her mother. She inched a step or two, leaning for his hand, begging his help. But John Fleming dared not come to meet her. He kept his arm outstretched, his fingers trembling, yet would not let halfway be enough.

"Help her," Mrs. Fleming cried.

Gail tried to inch another pace, but the muscles of her legs and back gave in and she fell. In the act of falling she was incredulous that her father had not attempted to save her. The incredulity showed in her face as she went down. She fell awkwardly and hurt her head.

"There." Mrs. Fleming crouched, flashing an angry glance to her husband. "Now perhaps you'll believe."

He crouched also, murmuring apologies because he should have saved her.

"Help get her back to bed." Mrs. Fleming's tone was impatient, scornful. "Goodness knows what they did to her in the hospital. But one thing's certain. We're not going to try it here."

John Fleming watched her tuck the covers. Then he said, "Perhaps she should go back there."

"What?"

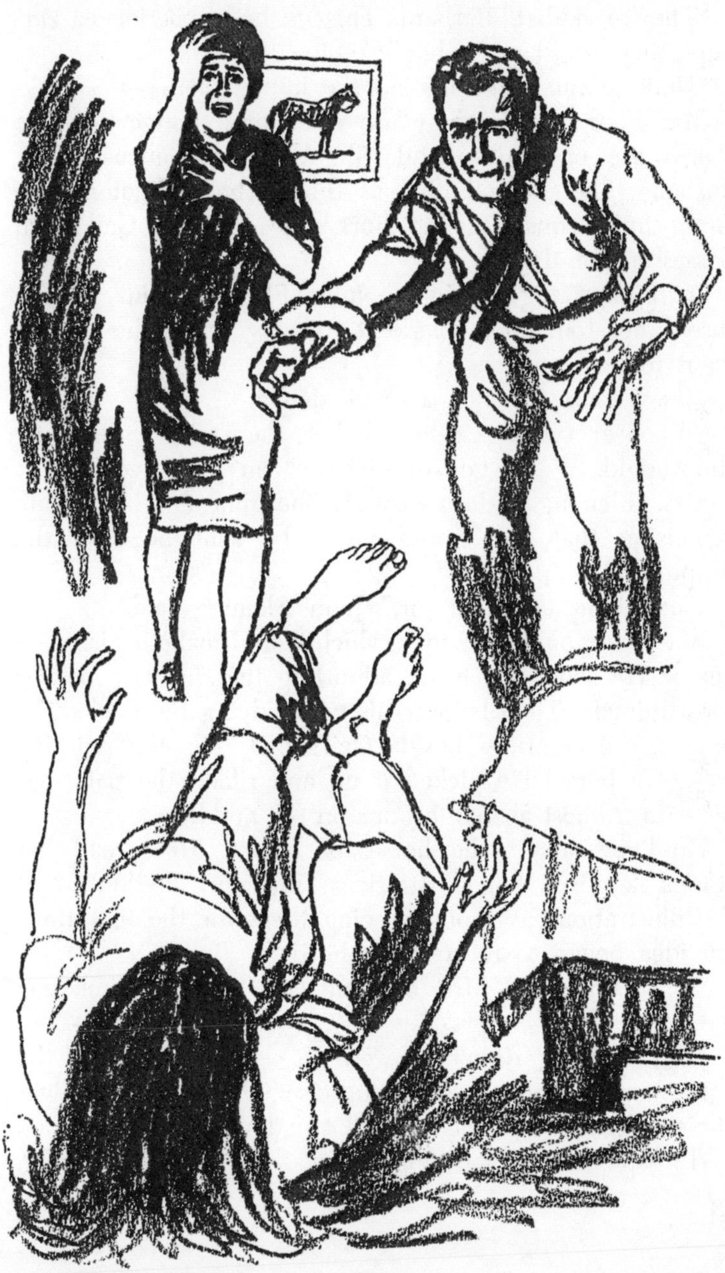

"They're skilled, Barbara. They've had experience. Perhaps they could make her."

"Nobody can make her do the impossible."

Mrs. Fleming brought warm water and sponge to bathe the bruise on Gail's head. She did not glance at her husband. She ignored him, as though he had joined Dr. Craig in a conspiracy to hurt. She touched Gail with possessive gentleness.

"I think Craig is right," John Fleming said. "We've fussed her too much, made it too easy until she doesn't want to try."

Mrs. Fleming flashed a quick denial.

"When everything's done for her, there's no reason why she should. We've got to give her an incentive."

Mrs. Fleming didn't answer. She murmured to Gail, promising that she would never be sent back to the hospital.

"Something to strive for," John Fleming said.

But what could they give which would make a girl walk again? He shook his head, admitting that he was looking for a miracle. Then he saw his wife tidying the books, the papers, the paintings beside Gail's bed. The top painting was of a horse. He picked it up and riffled the paintings beneath. Almost all had a horse in the middle.

He knew about the horse, of course. He'd read her stories, admired her illustrations. But now he looked at the illustrations as though seeing them for the first time. An idea began to form in his head.

"It's nearly ten," Mrs. Fleming said. "Isn't it time you left?"

John Fleming didn't answer. He looked again at the paintings and noticed something else. The horse was never alone. There was always a girl standing at its head.

He replaced the paintings. Now the idea was buzzing.

CHAPTER SIX

John Fleming took off his raincoat, hanging it on a peg behind the door. Then he took off his tweed jacket and put on the woolen cardigan which he wore in the office. Two of its leather buttons were missing. He moved around the littered desk to his swivel chair. He ruffled back his hair with a hand and stared at nothing, biting the knuckle of his right thumb.

Then he made up his mind and reached for the phone. One of the duties of a journalist is to know the people who matter. Not only councilors and local government officials, but local experts; farmers, shepherds, hedge-cutters, fishermen, each an expert in his own way and able to answer questions. John Fleming had his list of men who could be relied on to give authoritative answers.

"Teddy Leech," he said to the switchboard girl, letting her find the number.

Teddy Leech was a former point-to-point rider who trained steeplechase horses on Dartmoor. At the same time he bred ponies for sale and often brought young horses from Ireland for sale later. Generations of the Leech family had bred and trained and ridden horses. What Teddy didn't know about horses wasn't worth knowing, although that was all he knew. Talk to him about anything else—the Chancellor of the Exchequer or United Nations or C.N.D.—and he was ignorant.

The voice on the phone was Mrs. Leech. John recognized it at once.

"Hullo, Mrs. Leech. This is John Fleming of the *Weekly Advertiser*."

"Oh hullo," Mrs. Leech said. "You'll be wanting Teddy."

"Please," John Fleming said.

"He's in the yard. If you hang on a minute."

John hung on, hearing the faint echo as she called her husband. After a while Teddy's boots were on the flagstones. Then his voice was there, shouting because Teddy always shouted on the telephone. It seemed that he did not trust the GPO to carry his voice by wires. He shouted to make sure.

"Hullo, John. What you want for that old paper?"

"Not the paper, Teddy. Something personal."

There was a pause as Teddy sensed the urgency. Then he said, "Well, what can I do for you then?"

"A horse," John Fleming said. "I want a horse."

Teddy laughed. "You mean a pony."

"No. A pony wouldn't do."

"Got a good one here," Teddy said.

"No pony could be right." John remembered the illustrations. "This horse must be big, tall, black. It's got to look like a champion."

"You're asking something."

"I want it for my daughter," John Fleming said.

The pause was embarrassed, for Teddy Leech knew about Gail and what had happened to her leg. "Well, there's plenty of time. I'll have a look round."

"It's urgent," John Fleming said.

"But your young maid, it'll be years before she's fit enough to ride a thoroughbred."

"It has to be now," John said.

Teddy thought a moment. You could imagine him pulling his right ear, the way he always did. "Well, I got one here. Black, over sixteen hands. That ought to be big enough."

John knew that horses were measured by hands in the gypsy way. Each hand was four fingers, and each finger was an inch. This meant that Teddy's horse was over sixty-four inches in a straight line from wither to ground. Over five feet four.

"Quiet though," Teddy said. "Bought a few months ago for resale later on."

John Fleming sighed with relief. "It sounds fine."

"Seven years old and just coming to its prime. Come round and have a look."

John Fleming looked at the spike on top of his desk. The spike was a sharp piece of metal, standing up like a spear from a block of wood. Typewritten papers were stuck on it. They were the notes which correspondents had sent in from far-flung villages. Carefully he said, "There's one other thing."

Teddy guessed. He laughed as he said, "You mean—how much?"

"Yes," John Fleming said. He did not share the laughter.

"Well, seeing it's you. I wouldn't take less than two hundred and fifty pounds from anyone else, but seeing it's you, John."

John Fleming groaned.

"Too much, is it?"

"Yes," John Fleming said.

"I could come down a bit. Say two hundred and thirty pounds."

"Still too much. Much too much."

"Not for the kind of horse you want. How high you willing to go?"

61

John Fleming pinched the bridge of his nose. He was tired, depressed. His mind was muddled with thoughts of insurance premiums and mortgage repayments and income tax. "That's the trouble, Teddy. I can't go very high."

"How high?"

John Fleming hesitated, then went as high as he dared and higher than his wife would approve. "Fifty guineas."

"What?" Teddy was scornful. "You won't get a good horse for that. Ponies are fetching more."

"I know," John Fleming said. "But help me if you can, Teddy. It's very urgent."

During the day he phoned others who might be able to help. They all had horses which sounded all that Gail had imagined, but each owner wanted more, much more than fifty guineas.

"You'll never get what you want for that," they said.

John Fleming knew it was true.

In the evening he read Gail's stories again, absorbing her picture of the dream horse and realizing how improbable it was that he would ever find one. He sat in the armchair near the fire, looking at the television news but not thinking of it. The picture flicked from Downing Street to New York, from South Africa to India. None of the international news seemed to matter. The only important problem was here; the only insoluble crisis was in the bedroom where his daughter lay.

Barbara Fleming saw his anxiety. She came behind his chair, resting her forearms on the back and leaning to see what was on his knee. She was surprised. He'd seen the stories before, the illustrations before. She came around the chair to see what was in his face. She knelt beside him, hoping that what she saw in his face was not true.

She said, "You can't even think of it."

John Fleming looked beyond her to the television screen. The pictures were of politicians in Washington.

"For all kinds of reasons," Barbara Fleming said. "In the first place we can't afford it."

He knew she was thinking of the mortgage. They'd needed a high mortgage to buy the house. They were already struggling to meet the quarterly repayments.

"And in the second, we've nowhere to keep it."

"I could build a stable," John Fleming said.

"But you know what you are with tools. And the barn is tumbledown. Putting it right would cost a fortune."

About thirty pounds for timber and nails and screws and hinges. That was a fortune.

"Besides you know what happened last time." She was thinking of Topper. "An experience like that, we can't risk it again."

The screen flicked from one scene to another. From Washington to Paris. But still the faces were politicians. He'd seen them too often. He no longer believed anything they said.

"And even if we rented a field and built a stable and paid goodness knows what for a horse. Even then," Barbara Fleming said, "there's no guarantee it would work."

He looked at her for the first time. "It might."

"It wouldn't. It couldn't." She caught his hands and pressed them. "Don't think about it. You're looking for a miracle."

Their eyes met in a moment of deep tenderness. He thought she was probably right. She usually was. Yet as long as there was a spark of hope . . .

He said, "I've got to go on trying, Barbara. As long as there's any chance at all."

Two days later a lorry arrived with lengths of timber.

Gail saw it pull up and from her window she watched the driver and his mate unload the lengths. She was bewildered but her mother would not explain. Mrs. Fleming would only say, "Something your father wants to do." And that was worse than nothing. In the evening Gail asked her father and he said, "The barn. It's falling down. It's time I put it right."

It seemed plausible, but still Gail was not sure. "Why doesn't Mummy want you to do it?"

He darted a glance. "Did she say that?"

"No."

He seemed relieved. "Well, you don't know then. Not for sure."

"I do." Gail was surprised how slow adults could be. "I know Mummy doesn't want you to do it and you know it, too."

This time her father did not argue. Grimly he said, "It'll be done. We can't have a ruin near the gate."

During Saturday afternoon Gail watched him measuring and sawing, heard him hammering, then calling for a bandage when the chisel gashed his finger. On Sunday morning Mr. Jennings wandered over, attracted by the sounds of hammering and unable to resist. Jobs about the house were his favorite hobby. He was proud of his modern tools, ready to show off his electric drill like a youth showing off his motorcycle.

John Fleming welcomed him. At other times they had little in common; one interested in books and plays and local history, the other in four aways and Test matches and *Sunday Night at the Palladium*. But in times of emergency, when the car broke down or the kitchen needed painting, John Fleming welcomed assistance from anyone and Rod's father was the local expert.

"What's on then?" Mr. Jennings asked.

Mr. Fleming looked to the window, knowing that Gail was watching and listening. "The old barn was falling down."

"It still will if you go about it like that." Mr. Jennings laughed, ridiculing the efforts of an amateur. "Here. Let me give a hand."

Like his cheek, Gail thought. Yet she had to admit that as soon as Mr. Jennings took over, the work became swift and efficient. No more accidents. No more complaints about blunt saws or the head coming off the hammer. Her father became Mr. Jennings' assistant and by Wednesday evening the work was done.

The repair of the barn was the first mystery. Mr. Amos was the second.

Mr. Amos owned the farm on the other side of the hill. He had taken over the walled-in fields near Gorse Blossom and all the cattle which grazed those fields were his. Gail heard him talking with her father, hearing their voices without recognizing what they were saying. They had switched off the microphone in the living room, and that was fishy.

Only once could she be certain. Then Mr. Amos said as he went out, "We'll leave it like that then. You have it if you want it for the rent we agreed. But if nothing comes of it, I'll turn out a few bullocks. Fair enough?"

"Very fair," Mr. Fleming said.

Something was being planned. But Gail knew also that it was no ordinary secret. There was no suppressed excitement, as there was in the week before Christmas. Her father's face gave no hint of merry secrets which he would reveal if she asked enough questions. Her mother's expression was closed up, making it plain that she wanted no part in whatever it was.

Gail wondered why they didn't kiss and make up and

be as they usually were and as parents ought to be. She asked her mother, "What's wrong between you and Daddy?" Her mother answered, "Nothing, there's nothing wrong." In the morning she asked her father, "Why can't it be like it used to be?" But he was no more willing to admit what anyone who lived with them could see with half an eye.

He was in the bathroom, shaving with more than ordinary care because this was no ordinary Saturday. She could see him along the landing. He dipped the brush in hot water and gave himself a white beard. Then he pulled his face to one side and drew the razor down.

She asked, "Why have you got to go?"

"Because it's the races." He tilted his head, drawing the razor up his neck. "You know what that means."

Four times a year there were National Hunt races on the city racecourse. Each day he had to be there, phoning results for the London newspapers and making notes to prepare a feature for the *Weekly Advertiser*. He was not a racing man. He seldom had a bet. It was a family joke that when he did, he always lost. Yet he was happy on race days because working temporarily for London newspapers meant extra money. Their radiogram, refrigerator, washing machine had all been bought with money earned on race days.

Gail liked to see him happy, to hear him singing as he splashed his face. Yet she couldn't forget that last April he had taken her to the races, that he might never take her again. His singing stopped, showing he had thought of it, too. His eyes clouded as he dried his face. She saw that he was trying to think of something to put it right.

"Tell you what." He came out of the bathroom. His dressing gown was red, a gift from Mummy two Christmases ago. The striped legs of his pajamas showed beneath. "You got the daily paper there?"

"Yes," Gail said.

"Turn to the sport." He passed into the big bedroom and opened a drawer of the dressing table. He was rummaging for a shirt. "The racing. Found the entries for today?"

"Yes," Gail said.

"Tell you what then. Pick me a winner and I'll put you on a bet. You might win a fortune."

She ran her glance down the runners. So many names. So many trainers and jockeys. Then she recognized a name. E. A. Leech. He was the owner and trainer of a horse in the fourth race.

"Harvest Halo," she said.

Her father came to the doorway, straightening his tie. "That's Teddy Leech's."

"I saw it once," Gail said. "One morning, going to school on the bus. Teddy Leech was riding it beside the road."

"All right, four shillings on the Tote. How's that?"

His gaiety was an act, put on to prove that everything was as it used to be. She pretended to be convinced, then listened as he went down the stairs to an early lunch. Half an hour later he went out to the car, tooting twice in a kind of good-bye. Then he drove across the moor to the city.

Racing began at two o'clock and the first race was a seller, meaning that the winner must be put up for auction at a minimum of one hundred guineas. He didn't watch the race. He seldom did. He heard the official announcement of the first four horses and scribbled notes against their names on the race card. Then he crossed the paddock to the auction ring, listening to brisk bidding for the winner. The price went as high as 380 guineas, showing what chance he had of buying a miracle for fifty.

Meanwhile the loud-speaker said, "Calling the veterinary surgeon. Will he go to box nineteen in the racecourse stables, please."

John Fleming wondered what had happened. He wandered back to the press room where another journalist explained, "Second favorite in the last race. Pulled up coming into the straight."

"What happened?"

The other journalist shrugged. "Horse called Samalaya."

John Fleming found it on the race card. A ten-year-old gelding, trained in the Midlands. Its previous form was 1–1–3, meaning that it had won two races recently and had been placed third last time out.

"Pulled up dead lame," the other journalist said. "That's all you could see from the stands." He lit a cigarette and blew smoke in a mournful stream. "Pity though. Samalaya was a good one in his day."

John Fleming wrote the initials "p.u." against the name, meaning that when he telephoned results at the end of the day he would report that Samalaya "pulled up" in the seller. He did not think of it again until after the fourth race, when he met Teddy Leech in the paddock. Teddy's horse had fallen at the fifth fence.

"Bad luck," John Fleming said.

Teddy shrugged. It was part of the game.

"Bad luck for Gail, too," John said. "She picked it."

"She won't win a fortune today then." Teddy grinned at his own joke, then beckoned the journalist away from other people. "You hear about Samalaya?"

"Pulled up in the seller."

"Tendons gone," Teddy said. "I know the trainer. The owner, too. They're talking of putting him down."

"Shooting him?"

"No use to them now. It would take a year to get that leg right and by then he'd be too old for good races. But you— I was thinking about you."

John Fleming began to think of it, too.

"Samalaya would be cheap. Anything over the carcase price. They might listen to that."

John Fleming wondered how much a zoo would pay for a dead horse.

"Anything over thirty pounds," Teddy said. "And I tell you something else. Samalaya is the half-brother to Arkle."

John Fleming's eyes widened. Arkle was the champion steeplechaser, bred in Ireland and declared to be the best fencer of the century.

"Same sire," Teddy said. "That shows what quality Samalaya is."

John Fleming clenched his hands to hide their trembling. "I'd have to see him."

"Wait till racing's over. The secretary will get you in the stables."

"But Samalaya might be shot by then."

"I'll see the trainer," Teddy said. "I'll explain you'll give the horse a good home."

Winter darkness was creeping across the racecourse as John Fleming finished telephoning and came out of the press room. The racecourse secretary was waiting for him. They were old friends.

"I'll vouch for you, John," the secretary said. "They'll let you in the stables."

Only trainers and stable hands with stable passes were supposed to be admitted. But security was relaxed as the secretary accompanied John Fleming through the gates. Teddy Leech was waiting. So was the trainer of Samalaya.

"Jack Cray," Teddy Leech said and John Fleming nodded.

They moved down the dark path toward the second block of stables. The boxes were numbered, like rooms in a hotel. A chain of lights shone outside the boxes and other lights were shining inside. The top doors of some of the boxes were open. Stable hands were working in them. But one box was shuttered. No light showed through the cracks. It was as dark as a condemned cell.

Cray slid back the bolts. He opened the doors and reached for the switch. The horse started as the light came on. The sound it made was a grunt.

"That's him," Cray said.

John Fleming moved to the edge of the box. He saw the droop of the horse's head, the wet hessian strapped around his leg.

"You can go in," Cray said. "He won't move."

John Fleming did not need to go in. He had seen all he needed; Samalaya was big and almost black and a thoroughbred. But as he watched from the doorway he saw something else. Samalaya was in great pain. Samalaya needed someone, even someone with little money and no skill.

"Thirty-five," he said. "I couldn't go higher." Then he touched his inside pocket. "But I haven't got my check book."

"Your name's good," Teddy Leech said. "You can bring it in the morning."

"I can wait till then." Cray looked at the journalist a long minute. Then he said, "Teddy was saying. You want Samalaya for your daughter."

"That's right."

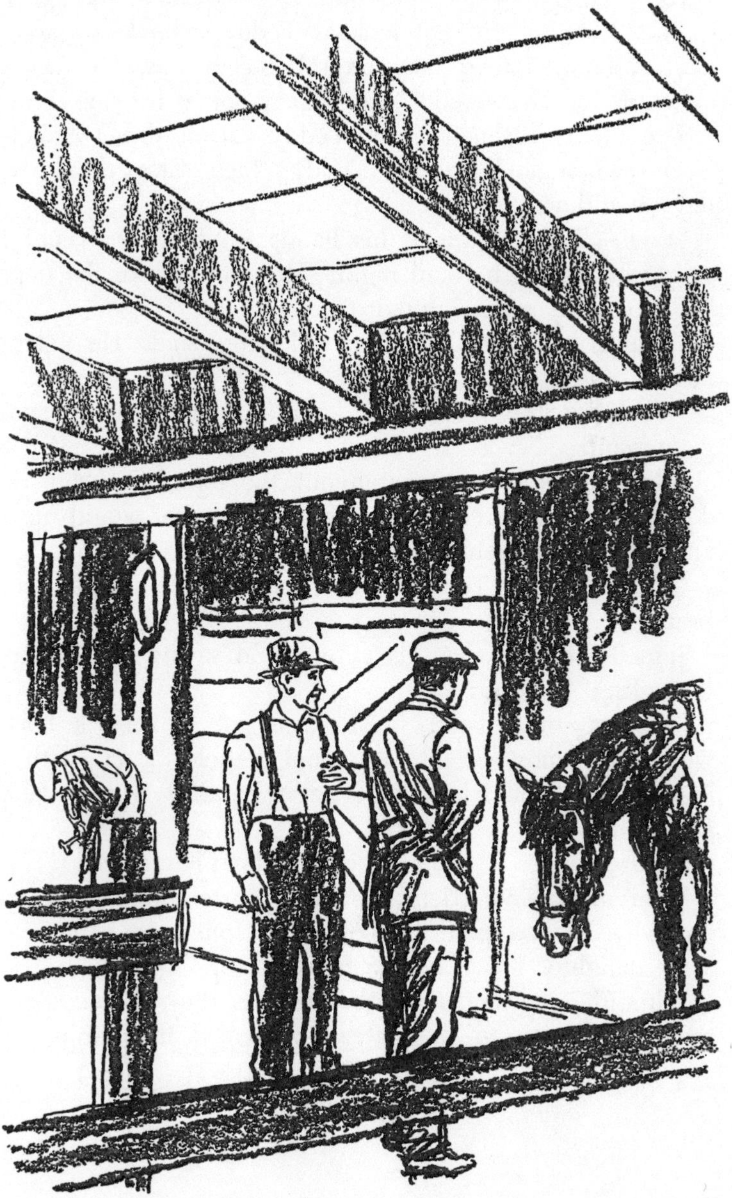

"She going to ride him then?"

John Fleming did not look at Teddy, who knew about Gail and understood how improbable it was. He looked away as he answered, "Yes. She's going to ride him."

The others listened to it. Teddy Leech didn't believe it and when he looked at Teddy's face, Cray didn't believe it either.

"Well," Teddy clapped his hands to show how cold it was, "can't stand here all night." He moved from the door. "I'll give you a hand tomorrow."

"Thanks very much," John Fleming said. He felt a novice among the experts.

"I'll bring the truck and lend all you need till you get organized."

John watched Cray switch out the light and bolt the doors. He wondered how many things he would need and what they would cost.

"Head collar," Teddy said, "and straw and hay and bran."

John imagined what his wife would say when she saw the bills.

"Blanket, too," Teddy said. "You got to keep a horse warm. But most of all you want a field. Even with a leg like that Samalaya will be a handful if you keep him in too long."

"I've arranged to rent a field," John Fleming said.

"You must have friends." Teddy darted a grin, knowing why he had plenty. "Well, you found your miracle. Your daughter got herself a class horse."

John Fleming smiled at the stars as they passed along the cinder path to the gates. It seemed incredible.

CHAPTER SEVEN

Early on Sunday morning John Fleming drove out of Gorse Blossom to meet Teddy Leech on the other side of the hill. He pulled up beside the horse truck and ducked out.

"Morning, Teddy."

"Morning, John. What's all the secret then?"

"Gail hasn't guessed. If she saw your truck, she'd soon put two and two together."

Teddy leaned to open the door of the cab. He waited as John climbed in. "What about your car?"

"Leave it there." John sat beside him. "No one will pinch my old crate."

Teddy gave it a long look and didn't argue. He let in the clutch and turned the truck toward the city.

Jack Cray was waiting at the racecourse. Stable hands were grooming and exercising horses, but none gave Samalaya a second glance. He hung his head over the half door, nuckering to other horses as they passed in and out. You could tell that he was bewildered. The routine of months had been broken. He felt left out.

John touched the horse's face, bringing his hand down the long bone to the nostrils. Samalaya lifted his head to get away from the hand. His ears were long and when he flattened them, his head lost all dignity. It became as ugly as a mule's.

"Where's the head collar?" Cray asked.

"Here," Teddy said.

Cray placed the leather collar over the horse's nose and ears, buckling the strap on the left cheek. He opened the door and pushed Samalaya aside. Teddy gave him a blanket. It was folded neatly into a long narrow shape, like the blankets which Mexicans used to carry diagonally across their chests. He placed the blanket on the horse's back, then opened it in two directions; over the wither toward the neck, then toward the croup and tail. He fastened it with a wide strap, placed behind the wither and buckled on the left side.

"What's that?" John asked, beginning to appreciate how much there was to learn.

"Surcingle," Teddy answered. "You can let me have it back when you buy your own."

Head collar and blanket, too, John thought. He wondered how much they would all cost and how he would make the extra money.

Cray crouched to the bad leg, his fingers pecking the tape which held the bandage. He unrolled the bandage and a wad of wet hessian fell away. They looked at the swollen leg.

"Hot's fire," Teddy murmured. "The heat is more important than the swelling."

John was appalled. "What happened?"

"Tore the tendons," Teddy answered. "Overstretched like overstretched elastic. It's what happens to steeplechasers."

John could not bear to look. "Cover it up," he said.

Cray held out a hand for cotton wool and a new bandage of crepe. Teddy gave them to him. He wrapped the cotton wool around the leg, then strapped it with the bandage. John noticed that the bandage was three inches wide. It stretched as the trainer pulled. He tied the tapes on the inside of the leg, where the horse could not bite the knot.

"That'll support the leg," Cray said. "It's sure to hurt going up and down the ramp."

He put a hand on the head collar and nodded to Teddy who opened the door. Samalaya lifted his head, suddenly proud and arrogant like an old actor putting on an act to show he was not finished yet. He walked firmly out of the loose box and pranced on the cinder path, as if trying to prove that he was as fit as he had been twenty-four hours before. He gave no hint of lameness as he passed between the boxes to the truck.

The ramp was already down. Teddy scattered a thin film of straw and Samalaya did not hesitate. He went up boldly. Cray tied the head collar, and when he came out, John helped Teddy to lift the ramp and to bolt it.

"Well, that's it then." Cray offered John his hand and they shook hands. "Take good care of him. He was a smashing horse in his day."

A minute later John was in the cab beside Teddy, and the truck was passing out of the racecourse to the Sunday streets.

"I'll give you some ointment." Teddy frowned as he drove. "Rub it in once a day, getting the heat out and the swelling down."

He stopped at a traffic light and thought of something else.

"No corn for six months. Corn is heating. It would make that leg worse. Just bran mash, made with cold water. Not wet, only damp. And hay, of course, and grass."

John clenched his hands. He was trembling, partly with excitement because this would be a great day for Gail; partly with alarm because he had assumed a responsibility which seemed to become the more formidable the more he thought of it. Owning Topper had been no preparation for this. Topper had needed little looking after. You'd just turned him out in a field and called when you wanted him. But John had seen enough this morning to know that looking after Samalaya would be a different matter.

"He'll settle down," Teddy said. "Make a fuss of him. That's what he needs most. And if there's anything you're not sure of, get on the phone. I'll do anything I can."

"Thanks, Teddy," John Fleming said.

They turned toward the moor and Teddy put his foot down, maintaining thirty miles an hour for ten miles. The Sunday roads were almost empty because this was November, and weekend cars did not venture to Dartmoor in winter. Some difference from July, John thought. Sunday roads then had been as busy as Piccadilly Circus.

"Those shoes," Teddy said. "They're racing plates. Made of steel, but as light as dancing shoes. You'll have to get them off. They'll pinch his feet else."

"Who'll do it?"

"The farrier who does mine," Teddy said. "I'll get him to come over."

They passed the Berry Brook and the isolated farm where the geese were watching, then the house with evil windows. They reached the fork which led to Gorse Blossom and John Fleming began to count the minutes. In ten minutes, in nine, in eight, Gail would look from her window and see the dream horse on the hill.

"This is it," he said.

Teddy drew up. "I don't see why."

John opened the door and jumped down. This was the place which Gail had remembered in the hospital and had painted often. The hawthorn tree there, the pile of rocks over there, and between them the heather. She had painted her horse standing in the heather, looking toward the hawthorn tree with the rocks behind. John knew precisely where Samalaya must stand. He looked down to the house in the valley. It was still. It gave no sign.

He helped Teddy to lower the ramp, then went up to unfasten the head collar. He talked to the horse in a voice that trembled. For the first time he realized how big Samalaya was. How strong. You could not shoulder him aside as you'd shouldered Topper. John turned the horse and brought him to the edge of the ramp.

There Samalaya stiffened, head high as he looked out. He had expected to see the familiar yard, the other horses trained by Jack Cray in the Midlands. He had supposed that was where they were going, for that was how it had been for years. A day traveling to the races, one or two days in a strange loose box, then back to the Midlands and the environment which he knew best. He had supposed he was going home.

But this wasn't home. This place was strange and he mistrusted anything strange. His head was high, his neck stiff. The thudding of his heart was loud.

"Come on," Teddy said. "It's cold waiting."

"Give him time," John answered. "Let him look around."

Finally Samalaya admitted there was nothing to fear. He moved down the ramp, his forelegs stumbling. Yet when he stepped from the ramp, he picked up his feet in a defiant dance, denying the pain. He moved toward the exact place on the hill. The wind got into his mane and tail. He snorted, his nostrils flaring like trumpet flowers. He held his head high, looking down the valley toward the house.

John held the head collar with his right hand. He raised his left, keeping it high in a signal until a white handkerchief answered from the porch. Then he knew Mrs. Fleming had seen.

Now she would be going up to their daughter's bedroom, talking to Gail, pretending that it was an ordinary Sunday. He imagined her lifting Gail's legs from the bed and waiting until the feet were firm on the carpet. Then he imagined her moving backwards to the window, telling Gail to come.

"I can't," Gail said. "It's too far, you know it is."

"Try," Mrs. Fleming said. "Hold on to this chair." She placed a chair halfway between the bed and the window. "But try, Gail. You've got to try."

Gail tried and swayed, one hand reaching for the chair. It was not near enough. Mrs. Fleming moved it until Gail could grasp the top bar.

"That's far enough, as far as I can go."

"Not today," Mrs. Fleming said.

"But it doesn't have to be the window. It's never been the window before."

"Today it must," Mrs. Fleming said.

But why, Gail thought? Only because you want to hurt me. Only because you're like the others, like Dr. Craig. Always telling me to try, then never satisfied.

She reached the window. She clutched the sill and leaned on her hands, her forehead prickling with heat, her eyes blurred by the tears of strain. She was panting. Her back, her legs ached to lie down. She clung to the sill, hating her mother for being on Dr. Craig's side. She opened her eyes, her head almost touching the glass. She straightened her head, flicking back her hair. It was a defiant gesture, showing her mother, showing Dr. Craig, showing everyone that they couldn't hurt her. She looked out of the window.

She saw the hill. She saw the hawthorn tree and the pile of rocks. In the middle there was a horse. The horse was standing erect and proud, looking toward the house. He was as noble as a king.

She closed her eyes and opened them again. But still she didn't believe it. She glanced to her mother, half expecting her mother to say, "What are you looking at?" For of course the horse wasn't there, couldn't be there. "Only your imagination," her mother would say. But Mrs. Fleming didn't shake her head.

Gail looked back, recognizing her father and Teddy Leech, then the vehicle on the track to Gorse Blossom. She laughed, realizing what her father had been planning; why he had been late home yesterday and early away this morning. Why he and Mr. Jennings had repaired the barn and why he had talked with Mr. Amos. But her laugh was not only a laugh. It broke in the middle and became something silly.

Tears were silly because they blurred her eyes so she couldn't see. She brushed a knuckle across her eyes and when she'd blinked twice, the horse was there again. He was a dark bay, not black as she'd imagined but near enough. He wore a yellow blanket and on one leg was a bandage. She was not surprised by that, for she'd seen other race horses with white bandages on their forelegs. She watched him fidget in a circle, picking up his feet as quick as dancing and whirling his tail.

"They're waiting for you to wave," Mrs. Fleming said.

Gail unfastened the catch and pushed the window. It opened outward, showing a slate sill with a crust of moss. She leaned and waved, keeping her hand moving until her father saw it and raised his in answer. Then she watched the horse turn toward the truck.

"You'll catch cold," Mrs. Fleming said.

Gail shook her head, begging her mother not to close the window, not to spoil it by having glass between.

"Your dressing gown then," Mrs. Fleming said. "And you mustn't stand too long."

Gail put up with the dressing gown, but she would not sit in the chair which her mother moved to the window. If she sat she would not see enough. She leaned on the sill, letting her forearms take much of her weight. She leaned as far as she dared, getting as near as possible to what was happening outside.

The truck came through the gate and stopped near the barn. Again her father and Teddy lowered the ramp. Again her father brought out the horse and again Samalaya hesitated a long time, rigid with looking and listening. Gail called and waved and Samalaya snorted, looking up to the window. Again the hammering of his heart was as loud as a drum.

Nobody noticed a bicycle coming down the hill. None realized that Rod Jennings was returning from the Mission Church until he appeared near the truck, leaning on his bicycle and watching incredulously as the horse came down.

"Out the way, lad," Teddy Leech said.

But Rod went away only to hide his bicycle. A minute later he was back, his eyes big and round; happy to stand and stare as John Fleming led the horse toward what had been the barn.

The loose box was ready. Its straw was deep, it had hay in one corner, a water bucket in another. Samalaya lowered his head, puffing the straw. When he was sure that it had not been soiled by other animals, he walked in and the straw hissed as he turned around. He came to the half-door, his eyes bold, his nostrils flared.

"Carrot," Teddy Leech said. "Give him diced carrot for tidbits."

John Fleming had no carrot. He slapped the horse's neck, promising to have carrots next time. Then he turned away, almost colliding with Rod who had crept close and wanted to ask questions. Where you get him? You going to race him? Who's going to ride him? I've always wanted to be a jockey. But John Fleming had no time for questions. He hurried back to the yard and looked up to his daughter's window. They stared a long time at each other.

In the bedroom Mrs. Fleming said, "The horse's name is Samalaya."

"It's what?" Gail asked over a shoulder.

"Samalaya. He ran in a steeplechase yesterday afternoon."

Gail tried the name. It was difficult to say. Her tongue stumbled over it. Suddenly she knew what the name must be. She called to her father, "His name's Sam."

Her father didn't hear, so she called again, "King Sam."

CHAPTER EIGHT

"What's he doing now?" Gail asked.

It was evening. The curtains were drawn, shutting out the cold moor and the frosted stars. The bedside lamp gave a warm glow.

Rod sat on the floor beside the bed, his back against the wall, his forearms on his drawn-up knees. They were eating grapes but not thinking of grapes.

"Munching hay," Rod said. "Me and your father, we bedded him down for the night."

Gail flashed a jealous glance. "My father didn't need you."

"He does," Rod said. "Stands to reason. He can't do it all alone."

"He can."

"He's got other work to do."

Again the jealous pang. Gail wanted to say, he's got me. I can help. I can do anything you can do. Only better. But when she spoke, she had forgotten the jealous pang. She said, "Isn't Sam marvelous though."

Rod didn't argue and that was proof. "Tomorrow he's going out in the field. With a New Zealand blanket to keep the weather out."

"Who said?"

"Your father said. Teddy Leech brought it over this afternoon."

Gail thought, you know so much. "You don't even know what a New Zealand blanket is."

A few hours ago that would have been true but Rod had been there when Teddy Leech brought it. He'd kept eyes and ears open. He'd seen Teddy demonstrate how it must be strapped and clipped. That made him an expert. "It's waterproof one side, gray blanket the other. It's got straps to keep it in position when a horse rolls. Sam could wear it for months and never shift it."

It sounded improbable, but Gail was afraid it was true. Rod's confidence was infuriating. Old show-off, she thought. But Rod had more to tell.

"In the morning your father's walking him down the field. Then out to graze all day and back to the box before dark. You'll be able to see from here if you get to a window."

"I can," Gail said. "It's easy. I did it today."

"Not that window." Rod picked a pip from his bottom lip. He held it between finger and thumb and flicked, aiming at the lamp. "You'll never see from here."

Gail's heart sank.

"You'll see him leaving and coming back, but you'll never see him in the field. Not from this side of the house." Rod nodded to the door. "You'll have to get along the landing to a window on the other side."

He made it seem easy. Gail looked at the door, judging how far.

"Reckon your mother will help," Rod said. "They might even get you a wheel chair or something."

Gail glared at the air of superiority; the assumption that a wheel chair would be necessary. Then she looked again at the door, admitting that along the landing to the window of the spare bedroom would be too far. Much too far.

She tried it in the morning and could not get beyond the landing. She leaned on her mother and her mother half carried her to a chair where she could see. She saw her father take off the head collar and close the gate. Sam turned away, head high as he looked around. Then he dropped his head, puffing the grass. He drifted his nose above the grass, choosing the best spot. Then he ate.

"He's settled down right away," Gail said.

Her mother asked, "Do you want to stay?"

"Of course. I want to be here all day."

"There won't be anything to see. Only a horse grazing."

Gail's glance was alight with astonishment. Didn't she understand?

"All right then." Mrs. Fleming smiled, because perhaps she didn't understand. "But you must keep wrapped up. It's bitterly cold."

She went down the stairs, pleased by Gail's delight in the horse yet worried because ownership meant new responsibilities. Especially financial. She'd known from the first that owning a horse would mean extra expense, but the list which John had prepared of the things they would need was longer, much longer, than she had expected. A new dustbin, for instance, keeping the bran safe from rats or mice. Who could have expected that?

Financial anxieties grew in her head until they overwhelmed her pleasure in Gail's delight. She spoke to herself as she moved about the kitchen, washing the breakfast dishes and cleaning the ashes of yesterday's fire.

John always leaves it to me, she thought. He leaves me to worry about the bills and how we're going to pay.

No sense of the value of money. He'd have been in debt long ago if I hadn't stopped his extravagances.

Even this house, she thought. It was he who wanted it. I was happier in the market town, near the shops and much more convenient. I had friends there. But he wouldn't admit we couldn't afford the house. He saw it and fell in love with it and couldn't wait to move in.

Ever since then we've been poor, much poorer than our friends or relatives have ever guessed. They've supposed that buying the house meant "old John" was doing very well.

Well, "old John" isn't, she thought angrily. "Old John" works too hard for too little money and every month there are worries about mortgage repayments and rates and life insurance and car insurance.

Now this, she thought in despair. A horse which needs good food, proper care, even a small field is more than we can afford. There'll be veterinary bills as well as merchants and blacksmith and saddler. We'll need bridle and saddle, blankets and head collar. We'll need good hay at over twelve pounds a ton.

I've worked it out, she told herself. John hasn't. He's never come face to face with it. But it'll cost sixty pounds for essentials, and one hundred and fifty pounds a year after that.

And for what? A broken-down horse which no one might ever ride. She wouldn't listen to the small voice in her head which said that Gail might ride and that if Gail ever rode, all the expense and time and worry would be justified. She shook her head, refusing to hope for a miracle. It's not fair, she thought. John leaves all the worrying to me. It makes me seem a kill-joy.

The thoughts were in her head all day, yet when John came home in the afternoon, she was resolved not to express them. It would be no use. It would only mean a quarrel and Gail would hear and be frightened. She made a pot of tea as he came in. Brightly she said, "You're nice and early."

He grunted as he took off his coat and the grunt told her that his day was not over yet. "Parish council meeting this evening."

That meant he would travel to some remote village and sit in a cold schoolroom while members of the parish council discussed the need for a new SLOW sign. Or vandalism among the young. Or the fluoridization of water. Parish council meetings were what he hated most.

He sat in the chair beside the fire, looking up as Mrs. Fleming brought him a cup of tea. He looked into her face, seeing the thoughts which she had resolved to hide.

"You're worried about something."

"It's all right."

"I can see you are." He caught her hand as she tried to turn away. "We've been married nearly twenty years. Do you think I can't tell?"

"If you must know." She tilted her head, risking a quarrel. "I'm worried about how much it will cost."

"Teddy Leech is helping."

"But we can't borrow from him forever. The head collar, blankets, even the bandage. They're all his. Sooner or later we'll have to buy our own."

He nodded as he sipped his tea. "I've been thinking about it."

"But not like me," she cried. "You haven't come face to face with it."

"I have." He sipped again. "Today I did something about it."

She looked at him, half expecting some wildly optimistic plan which everyone knew would never work. One of his plays, for instance. He'd been writing plays for years. Stage plays, radio plays, television plays; sending them away with high hopes, then refusing to give in when they were rejected.

Now she was half afraid that he would say, "I've had a new idea for a play. A radio play, they're in big demand. It might earn us a hundred pounds or more."

But something in his manner suggested that this time his plan was down-to-earth. "I've told the London papers. Anything they want done, any time of the day or night."

She began to realize what that would mean. He would be available at any hour of the twenty-four, seven days a week. She looked at the deep lines in his face, realizing how tired he was. "But you'd never be home. You'd be called out in the middle of the night."

"They pay well, Barbara." He put his arm around her, drawing her to the arm of his chair. "And they like to have local men available. I know one who makes ten pounds extra a week."

It sounded marvelous. She looked at him, wondering if he was determined enough, consistent enough. "If you can do that. We'd have no worries then."

His smile was tight. He understood her doubts. "This time I'll prove it. I don't care how many hours or what it costs. As long as Gail keeps Sam."

The following day he had his chance to prove it. Two prisoners broke from Princetown prison. They were free on the moor and both were dangerous. One at least was believed to be armed. This made them newsworthy, for desperate men might rob houses, steal cars, perhaps hold-up some wanderer on the moorland. The telephone shrilled with demands for information.

Every London newspaper wanted details, trusting him to use his contacts and local knowledge. His car roared out of Gorse Blossom toward the prison. He came back two hours later to phone preliminary reports for the first editions. Then he left again, using public telephones during the night to keep in touch with Fleet Street. In the gray light of morning he telephoned his home.

"John," Mrs. Fleming said, "are you all right?"

"Never mind me. How's Gail?"

"Fine. Worried about you. The first thing she asked was if you'd come."

"As soon as I can. But it won't be this morning."

"Why not? Where will you eat? Get a shave?"

"I'll eat in the town," John said.

Mrs. Fleming imagined the worst. He would have beans on toast and let that be enough. He'd never been interested in food or considered regular meals important.

"I must get to the *Advertiser* office by nine," John said. "The old man won't like it if I put the London papers first and let the *Advertiser* slide."

She knew that was true, but her concern for him wanted to protest. Then she thought of something else. "Is it over? Have they caught the men?"

"No sign," John said. "Only rumors. Everyone seems to think they're still on the moor."

"When will you be back then?"

"This afternoon with any luck. If only for an hour or two."

Long enough for a good meal, she thought, followed by a doze beside the fire. Then the telephone would shrill again and the London newspapers would be frantic.

"Well, look after yourself."

She put down the phone, still worried because when he was tired he smoked too much. Then she realized what his absence would mean. She stared at a framed print on the wall. She was horrified.

"Mummy."

She looked up to the bedroom. She guessed that Gail had heard half the telephone conversation and wanted to know the other half.

"It's all right," she said on the stairs. "Daddy will be home later. He's been busy earning a windfall."

"Have they caught the men?"

"Not yet." Mrs. Fleming entered the bedroom. "But let's hope they do today. Otherwise Daddy will be out again all night."

A voice in her head said, but that's what you wanted. You wanted the extra money. But the extra money did not seem so important now.

Gail's eyes were wide and earnest. "If he won't be home, who's going to feed Sam?"

Mrs. Fleming thought, heaven help me. I've never been near such a big horse. Only Topper. And I was nervous even of Topper. She tried to smile as she said, "I am."

Gail watched her. "Well, if you're sure."

"Quite sure," Mrs. Fleming said.

But she remained a long time in the bedrooms, pretending to be tidying, postponing the inevitable. Not until reproach showed in Gail's eyes did she tighten her courage and say, "I'm going now." Then she kept walking before her courage ran out.

She knew that Gail was listening as she went down to the hall. She put on an old coat and opened the door to the path. She looked up, sensing movement at the window. Gail was there.

Mrs. Fleming stared at the pale face, realizing that for the first time her daughter had walked unasked, unaided, with no one in the room to give confidence or encouragement. For a moment her astonishment was such that she forgot where she was going and why. Then she thought, Gail doesn't trust me. She's watching to be sure.

The top door of the loose box was closed. She slid back the bolt and opened the door and suddenly Sam was there, his head big and impatient because usually his top door was opened earlier than this. He shuddered his nostrils at the morning air. He wagged his head up and down, showing he was hungry.

"All right," Mrs. Fleming panted. "You've got to be patient. I don't know where everything is."

She found the bran, then the galvanized bowl which her husband had bought. There was a rime of old mash around the inside, showing how much. She filled the bowl as far as the rime and carried it to the tap. For half the winter this tap was frozen and useless, but Mr. Jennings had wrapped it in straw and hessian and so far this winter it had escaped the frost. She dribbled in a little water and mixed the bran. Shreds of the brown stuff got beneath her fingernails. She made an exclamation of disgust because she was proud of her nails.

Then she carried the bowl to the box and stood a long time, summoning what remained of her courage. Stand back, she thought. You silly thing. You're stopping me getting in.

Sam didn't understand. He thought she was teasing him with the promise of food. He stretched his neck, his ears flat. She thought him an ugly brute. When stretching his neck was not enough, he toed his door, rattling it imperiously.

Barbara Fleming glanced to the gate, hoping for Teddy Leech, for Mr. Jennings, for Rod, for the postman even. Anyone would do. But the school bus had left. So had Mr. Jennings. The postman would not be here for an hour and

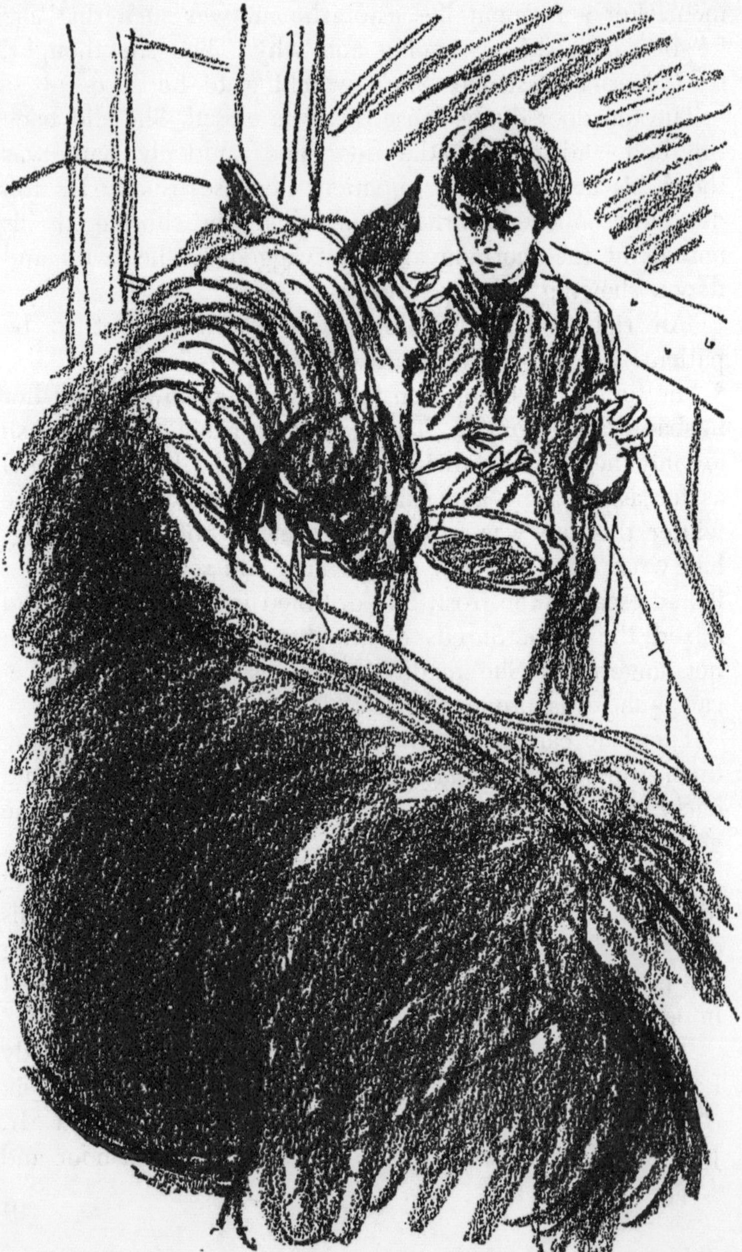

might not come at all. No one can help you, Barbara Fleming thought.

She slid the bolt and opened the lower half of the door. She forced herself to cross the threshold. Sam moved with her toward a slate shelf, about eighteen inches high and supported by pillars of stones. She placed the bowl on it and Sam dropped his head. She backed out, stooping for the water bucket without taking her eyes from the horse. He glanced at her, the bran freckling his nose. He seemed surprised by the fuss.

Barbara Fleming closed the door, listening to the knocking of her heart. She thought, I must be the biggest coward. Yet she was not ashamed. Beneath her trembling was a strange elation, because she had overcome her fears and survived.

So far, she thought grimly. There's the water bucket yet.

She filled the bucket and opened the door and leaned to place it in a corner. Sam looked at her again but seemed not to be thinking of her. He was thinking of his food. He ducked his head, his jaw moving with a loud, marching rhythm. This time she did not hurry to close the door. She looked at the bandaged leg, wondering if the pain was as great as Teddy Leech had said it must be. Sam gave no sign of it. The only hint was the way he stood with the bandaged leg forward, resting it and taking much of his weight on the other foreleg.

Poor old fellow, Barbara thought.

She closed the door and bolted it, delighted by her success. She came from the stable and waved to the window, showing Gail that it was all right. She went indoors and washed her hands, brushing the shreds from her fingernails. Then she climbed the stairs, her excitement smiling because she had been more frightened than Gail would ever understand.

"It's all right," she said. "Sam's having his breakfast. He loves that bran."

Gail did not move from the window. "But you can't leave him there. Not in his box all day."

Mrs. Fleming remembered what Teddy Leech had said. A horse confined too long could become dangerous.

"He likes his field," Gail said. "And the exercise. It's what he needs."

Barbara Fleming thought, I can't. I've already done more than I thought possible. She spoke sharply. "Daddy will do it."

"He won't be home till this afternoon. Perhaps not before dark."

That was true. Barbara Fleming thought, I'll ring, tell him to come at once. Then she realized that wouldn't be fair. He was already busy; the editor was already suspicious that he might neglect the *Advertiser*. Sadly she admitted that this was no isolated emergency. It would happen again, tomorrow perhaps; whenever John Fleming had to do extra work for the London papers.

She looked at Gail. Almost the truth came out. Almost she said, "I'm afraid." But her daughter's eyes were big, bewildered by the fuss because all she had to do was lead the horse out of the box and along the road to the field.

It sounded easy. A child could do it. Rod would do it if he had the chance. Gail would do it if she could walk. Mrs. Fleming was ashamed of her alarms.

"You're right about Daddy." She tried to keep her voice bright, as though it didn't matter. "He'll probably be much too late. I'll go and do it now."

She passed out of the bedroom. She was at the top of the stairs when Gail said, "Don't forget the blanket."

Mrs. Fleming was transfixed by horror, knowing what it meant but trying to deny it. Desperately she said, "He's wearing one, the yellow one."

"That's no use," Gail said. "It blows about in the wind and slips when he rolls. He needs the New Zealand blanket in the field."

Barbara Fleming had watched her husband put it on, an elaborate affair of straps and clips. She thought, the straps go between the back legs. I'll never do it. In a panic she said, "The yellow one will have to do."

"He'll catch cold," Gail said. "He'll die. He's not used to bitter cold."

Barbara's patience exploded. All this fuss for a horse. But she knew that Gail would never forgive if she did not put on the special blanket. She went down the stairs again, and when she passed toward the stable she knew without looking that her daughter's face was at the window. Not fair, she thought. I was born in a town, not used to the country. It's not fair to expect me to go in there and risk it.

The outer covering of the New Zealand blanket was green. She studied the straps and clips, working it out in her mind. Then she took diced carrot from a paper bag and found the nylon rope which her husband used for tying the head collar to the staple. She opened the door.

Sam looked at her and at once she knew that his look was different. His bowl was empty. He had no food to distract him. He stared as though seeing her for the first time. His head jerked up in mistrust. He looked down his long nose and moved back a pace. The swish of his tail was like the swish of wheels in heavy rain.

"Sam," she said in entreaty.

She held out a cube of carrot with one hand and reached for the head collar with the other. He took the carrot and flinched up his head, but not far enough to break away. He nudged for more while she fumbled for the metal rectangle beneath his chin. She threaded the rope through, stumbling from him as he butted.

"All right," she panted, "wait a minute. The more you keep bumping, the longer it will take."

She got the rope through and gave him more carrot. Then she found the staple in the wall and tied him to it. Sam tried to back away. He sidled across the box, reducing the gap through which she could reach the door.

She thought, I'm going to be trapped. Her terror leaped and became a taste in her mouth. She thought she was going to be sick. In a frantic moment she began to pray. She was praying as she passed him, her shoulder brushing his side. He flinched from her touch and suddenly she realized that he was frightened, too.

Both of us, she thought. Both frightened silly.

She tried to make a joke of it as she picked up the green blanket and went back. She placed it on the slate shelf and gave another cube of carrot. Then she screwed her courage and ducked under his head to the left-hand side. She saw the straps of the surcingle. She unfastened it and at the momentary tightening around his girth, Sam flattened his ears and kicked. A back leg was a blur. It was over before she realized. She thought, you could kill me. One kick would be enough.

She remembered how John had taken off the yellow blanket. Folding it inwards, from the neck, then from the croup which she called the back-end. Doing it slowly, because if you dragged it off the horse might jump. Well, I don't want you to jump, Barbara Fleming thought. You're frightening enough just standing. She took off the yellow blanket so slowly that Sam stamped in impatience.

She placed it on the slate shelf and picked up the green.

It was heavy. The need to reach up made it heavier. She struggled it over the high back, knowing that she did it wrongly, expecting him to kick in protest. But Sam only made an exasperated sound.

You're a good boy, Barbara thought. Then she began praising him, murmuring extravagant praises as she reached for the strap around his girth, then for the straps between his back legs. She clipped one and moved behind him in a wide arc. But Sam was suspicious of a movement which he could not see. He tried to look around as she took the last strap and fastened it. Then she passed in a wide arc again, smearing her hands down her hips because they were so wet.

She unfastened the rope from the staple and Sam moved with her to the door. She opened it with one hand, holding him with the other. But his eagerness to get out was too strong for her right hand. He blundered the door wide, dragging her to the yard.

She knew that Gail was watching, but she dared not look up, dared not think of anything except the great feet stamping near. Sam knew the way to go. He led her to the gate, refusing to wait while she opened it. He bumped it with his chest. She had to lean against it, pushing it wide with her back and holding the rope with both hands. Then they were through and the gate was slowly closing.

Sam moved sideways, his head inclined toward her, his back feet stepping high like a circus horse. For perhaps twenty yards he pretended that he wanted to break away, that walking was not fast enough for a thoroughbred which had won so many races. But as they turned the bend away from the house, his head came down until it was below her shoulder. The lilt went out of his legs.

His feet became quiet. Once he stumbled, ducking his head toward his bad leg.

Barbara Fleming realized what he was telling her. His leg was hurting. He had play-acted a while, but now he was paying for it. His change of mood touched her heart and she was murmuring encouragement as they reached the gate. He lifted his head then, recognizing the field. She opened the gate and unbuckled the head collar. She thought he would gallop, perhaps kicking his back legs in celebration. But he walked away quietly, his shallow feet squelching the mud which showed where other animals had gathered. He didn't give her a glance as she closed the gate. He dropped his head and grazed.

All the fears leaked away, leaving her weak and happy. She leaned on the gate, feeling the cold wind in her face. She said, "You're a very sensible gentleman," not mocking herself for talking aloud to a horse. Then she added, "Of course you need that blanket. This wind is lazy."

"Lazy" was the Dartmoor word for a cold wind. Too lazy to go around, so it went through you. That was the local joke.

She walked jauntily toward the house, waving to Gail as she turned the bend. When she was near enough she called, "It's all right. He was as good as gold." It seemed that the minutes of terror in the loose box had never been.

She went up the stairs and helped Gail to a window from which she could see the horse. But this time she did not turn away, as though a grazing horse was nothing much to see. She leaned beside her daughter, watching Sam drift his nose above the grass. For a while he grazed, then lifted his head, his ears sharp and listening. It seemed he had heard something. He was looking toward the window, as though he knew they were watching.

Gail raised a hand, signaling to him. Sam stared and chewed for perhaps a minute. Then he dropped his head again and Gail lowered her hand.

"Do you always wave to him?" Mrs. Fleming asked.

"Of course," Gail said. "He knows I'm here."

For the first time Mrs. Fleming appreciated the link which was forming between her daughter and the horse. She pressed Gail's shoulder and went down to the kitchen and all she had to do before her husband came.

John Fleming came at three o'clock; too tired to sleep, too hungry to eat the meal which she had prepared. She had a cup of tea ready, but he only sipped it. He hurried up the stairs, not answering when Mrs. Fleming called, "You haven't even finished it."

He went into the spare bedroom where Gail sat at the window. He joined her in looking out to the field.

"Had his head down all day," Gail said. "He really loves that grass."

"Long time since he had any," John Fleming said. "Horses in training get artificial foods. That's what they need. But grass is their natural food and grazing all day, that's one long holiday for Sam."

They looked at the darkening sky, realizing that the twilight would be shivering. He said, "I'll bring him in soon. Although with that blanket he's warmer than I've been all day."

Then he realized. He glanced to the door as Mrs. Fleming brought in a tea tray. She said, "I've got to follow you around." But he didn't look at the tray or at the cup which she held out.

He said, "Who put Sam out this morning?"

The answer came from Gail. "Mummy did."

John Fleming stared at his wife. He still couldn't believe it. "You even put the blanket on? With all those straps and clips?"

Mrs. Fleming stooped over the tray, cutting his favorite cake in the hope of tempting him. But he would not let her cut the cake. He put an arm around her, drawing her toward him. She wore a flowered apron and a pale green dress. She looked beautiful, more beautiful to him than she had ever been in what were supposed to be her young, her best years. He held her close, half laughing because he knew what it had cost her.

Barbara Fleming was laughing, too. She ducked her head against him as she confessed, "I was terrified."

CHAPTER NINE

Gail recognized the car, the sheepskin jacket, the gray hair waving in the wind. She called as he came into the hall.

"Dr. Craig. Have you seen him?"

"Seen who?" the doctor asked. Then he added to her mother, "Good morning, Mrs. Fleming. Your daughter scarcely gives me time to get inside."

Gail was amazed by the stupidity of adults. You'd think a man clever enough to be a specialist would also be clever enough to know what she was talking about.

"Sam." She struggled from the window to the door. "Have you seen Sam?"

Mrs. Fleming appeared on the stairs. "Give the doctor time. He's only just come."

Gail made an impatient sound. It was typical of the way adults neglected the important and wasted time on good-mornings, how-are-you's. She looked beyond her mother to the doctor coming up. Accusingly she said, "He's in the field. You could have seen as you came down the hill."

Her reproach was a giveaway. It showed how she had been longing for him to share her delight in Sam.

"Can I see from here?" Dr. Craig reached the landing.

"If he's anything like your dream horse, he must be something to see."

"He's exactly like it," Gail said. "But the field's on the other side. You'll have to help me to the spare bedroom."

Her excitement was imperative. She held out an arm to him, the other to her mother.

"Can't you make it alone?"

For a moment her sun went in, sensing his disapproval. Resentment clouded her excitement. Always expecting me to do more, she thought. Never satisfied. Then her arm went around him and she lurched through the doorway of the spare bedroom. On the way her mother said, "She's made great progress. But all the way from her room to this one, it's much too far on her own."

They reached the window. Gail dropped into a chair and Dr. Craig leaned beside her.

"There." Gail pointed. "Isn't he marvelous?"

Dr. Craig peered a long time at the bandaged foreleg. He guessed the bandage was ominous.

"Marvelous," he said.

Gail's glance was quick, wondering if he meant it. His expression looked as though he did. Then she pushed the window wider and said, "Watch."

She leaned forward and called, but Sam gave no sign. She called again and for a moment it seemed that Sam still did not hear. Then he lifted his head abruptly, as though he'd been dreaming and the voice had just got through. He looked toward the house. His head was long and lean, his ears were sharp.

"He knows," Gail said. "We talk to each other every morning."

Dr. Craig smiled. "You mean you talk to him."

"Not only," Gail answered. "He talks to me. Watch.

He's waiting for me to call something. And when I don't, you hear what he says."

Sam watched the window a long minute. Then he moved to the wall, getting as near as possible. The granite wall was only as high as his chest. His chest looked broad enough to push the top stones down. His listening was asking her to call again. When she did not, he distended his nostrils and nuckered.

It was not a neigh. It was a confidential sound, impatient yet plaintive.

"Don't keep him waiting," Mrs. Fleming said.

Sam agreed with that. He nuckered again, telling her off. They laughed, for you could put words to this sound. It seemed that he was saying what-do-you-keep-me-waiting-for?

"I told you," Gail cried in delight.

Then she called to Sam, congratulating him on being the best horse in the world. Sam wasn't going to argue about that. He watched for as long as the window stayed open. Then he dropped his head and mooched along the grass. They saw that his ears were still listening.

"Anyone ridden him yet?" Dr. Craig asked, turning from the window.

"Not yet," Mrs. Fleming answered. "His leg isn't ready."

Dr. Craig looked back to Gail with a smile. "Two left legs . . . getting better together. You want to watch out, Windy. Or Sam will be ready before you are."

Gail didn't answer the smile. She looked down. The doctor had put into words her secret fear. She'd been afraid for weeks that Sam would be ready long before she was fit enough. Then somebody else would ride him. Her father or Teddy Leech. Or worse still, Rod Jennings. She thought, I couldn't bear that. Not Rod.

It wouldn't happen. She was sure of it. Something

would happen. She had no idea what. Something would happen to show everyone that her left leg was almost ready. Two days later it happened.

Her father took Sam to the field half an hour earlier than usual. She got out of bed to watch them leave the yard, straining to see for as long as they could be seen; then opening the window despite the cold to hear the clop of Sam's unshod feet. She looked to the bedroom door, impatient for her mother to help her to the spare bedroom. But Mrs. Fleming was busy downstairs.

"You must be patient." The voice from below was sharp. "And get back to bed. You'll catch cold."

Gail stayed at the window long enough to wave goodbye to her father's car. Then she struggled back to the bed and wrapped an eiderdown around her shoulders, listening to her mother pass along the stone-flagged passage to the cold room which had been the dairy. Then she heard it.

In the first flash of astonishment she didn't realize what it was. It was followed by a drumming sound. She cried "Sam" and heard again the shrill scream.

"Mummy."

Mrs. Fleming did not hear.

The drumming was louder. She thought that Sam was being chased, perhaps by dogs. She cried again for her mother, then moved to the door. She had only one idea; to get to the spare bedroom and to shout, frightening away the dogs.

She caught the architrave of the door, leaning on it, panting so loudly that the sounds of her fright filled the room. She looked along the landing, summoning her strength. She stumbled forward, holding the banister rail. She reached the door of the spare bedroom.

Now the drumming was louder. She heard a rhythmic

grunting and realized that it was Sam, galloping despite the pain in his leg. She thought, they'll kill him. She imagined dogs, great alsatians, chasing him like wolves, their teeth bared as they tried to pull him down.

She moved through the doorway, clinging to the door, hating the stupidity of her left leg. She dragged it across the room and reached the window and looked out. Sam was galloping with mane streaming, his tail flying like a banner. He pounded away from her, not hearing her desperate cry. He thundered toward the opposite wall and looked over it to the moor. He shrilled the scream again.

Gail looked up the moor and saw wild ponies. They had come across the skyline, looking for a sheltered valley. Their heads were up, their ragged manes were blowing. They were looking down the valley, as surprised by Sam as he was excited by them.

"Whatever is it?" Mrs. Fleming hurried in. "What's Sam so frightened of?"

"Not frightened," Gail said in relief. "He's seen the moorland ponies. He's showing off."

Sam showed off again, turning with a buck and a backward thrust of his heels. He galloped toward the window, his neck arched, his head proud. His nostrils were steaming.

Then Mrs. Fleming understood. "All horses were herd animals once. They like company. And Sam wants them to come and see what a wonderful fellow he is."

The ponies lost interest. They dropped their heads, scrounging whatever they could find in shriveled heather and bracken. They did not come down the hill toward the horse in the field. They maintained their independence, ignoring the show-off who thought he was the best horse in the world.

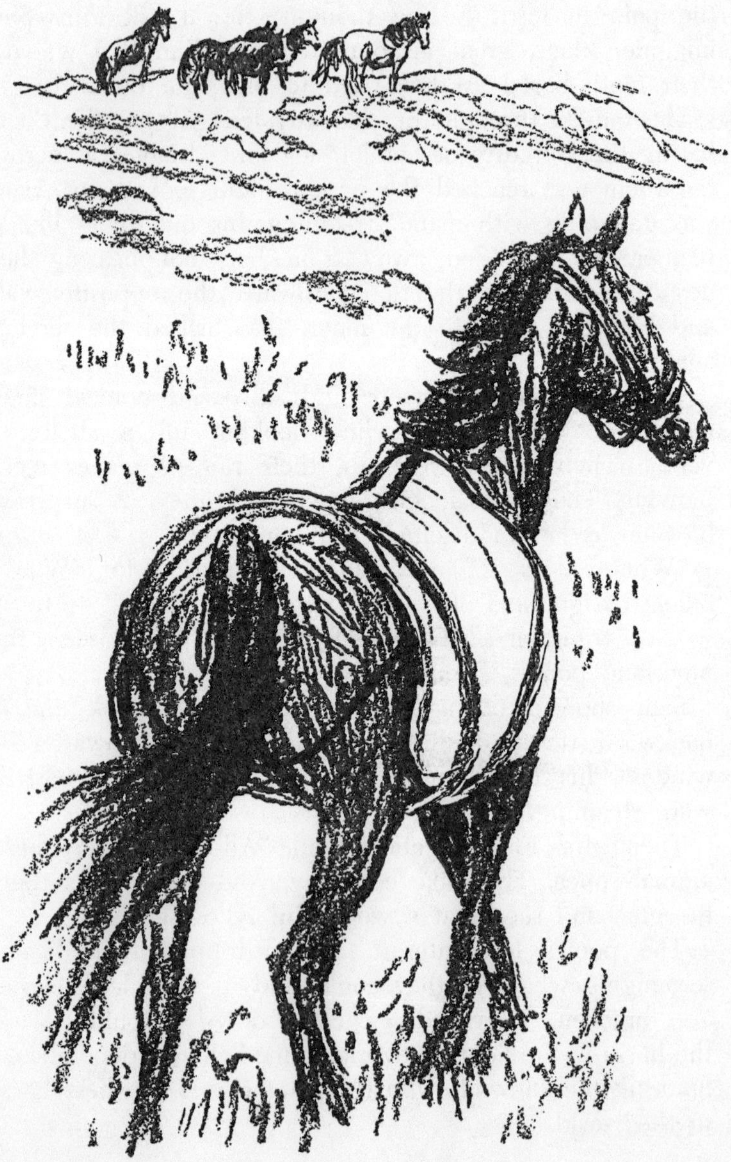

For a while Sam was indignant. He trotted up and down, looking out to the moor and shrilling a scream that commanded them to come. Finally he tired of the one-sided game. He shrugged, and turned his back on them, making them ragged ponies. Gypsies, tramps. Not worth another thought.

Peace came back to the valley. It seemed incredible that only five minutes before its quiet had been torn by shrill excitement.

"He's all right now," Gail said. "He must have wondered where those ponies came from."

But Mrs. Fleming had forgotten the horse. She was looking at her daughter, realizing what had happened. Her incredulity asked, "How did you get here?" But she already knew the answer. Alarm for the horse had shown Gail that she could do the impossible.

"That's a kind of milestone," Mrs. Fleming said. "You know you can do it now."

There was another milestone before the end of the month. Rod Jennings was the cause.

He shocked his mother by getting out of bed an hour earlier than he needed. As his mother said, "I couldn't believe me eyes, till I realized where he was going." Rod came to Gorse Blossom, spending the hour in helping Mrs. Fleming to feed Sam and put on the blanket and to walk him to the field. In the evening he was back again. All day Saturday he was working in the stable, forking manure to the heap in the yard, then scattering new straw.

Gail watched from the window, feeling helpless and useless and furious. Jealousy was the spark which lit her determination to reach another milestone.

She opened her chest-of-drawers, then her wardrobe. She found warm clothes; woolen jersey, jeans, thick socks.

Then she got to the door and looked down the stairs. They seemed steep and dangerous. Only fifteen, she told herself. I've counted them and fifteen stairs, that's nothing.

She clung to the banister and got down a step, taking her weight on her right leg. She gripped the banister sticks and got down another step. Two, she thought, only thirteen to go. But thirteen was supposed to be unlucky. She hurried to get down another step, and when it was twelve she laughed at herself, because thirteen could not really be unlucky. It was merely superstition.

One more step. Then she stumbled, frightened by the sea sounds in her ears. The stairs blurred. She sat and put her head in her hands, compelling the sea sounds to go away. She would not give in. She slid down the remaining stairs, still sitting, her hands helping to take each bump.

She reached the last stair and looked along the hall to the living room. It seemed she had come down to another world. She thought, I've done it. It didn't matter that she would have to get up again or that getting up would be worse.

She was sitting on the last stair when the living room door opened and her father appeared.

"It's all right." Gail flicked back her hair. "Don't help me."

Her father didn't seem to hear. He stooped, his hand under her arm.

"No, don't," Gail begged. "You watch. I can get to the front door easy."

She managed it but only just. She leaned against the door, laughing because she had escaped the restrictions imposed by habit and by fear.

"Why did you try it?" Mr. Fleming held her, frightened

by what might have happened. "On your own. You could have fallen."

"That'll show him," Gail said.

"Show who?"

Gail didn't explain. She said, "That'll show him I'll soon be doing it myself."

John Fleming shook his head in bewilderment. "As long as you don't try it again."

"I will," Gail said. "I'll try it every day until I'm good enough."

A week passed before she was good enough. Then the front door became the important barrier. When it opened and her father helped her through, she felt that another milestone had been passed. She sat in the porch, admitting that for a while this must be far enough.

But not for long. On Saturday afternoon she said she was ready. She leaned on her father's arm and crept down the path to the stable. There was triumph in her eyes.

Rod came from the box to the manure heap. He saw her coming down the slope and his astonishment was a kind of reward. He leaned on the fork until she was near. Then he said, "Good old Windy. You're doing fine."

She hadn't expected praise. She'd expected him to be jealous, protecting what he was doing from her interference. The glee went out of her face. She was ashamed, realizing that Rod hadn't wanted to take the horse from her. He had been merely doing what needed to be done.

"Hullo, Rod," she said. It was the most polite greeting they had ever exchanged.

For the first time she saw the stable; the partition of new wood which divided the box from that part of the barn which had become a store for bran and hay and straw. She saw the new straw which Rod had forked in; the shreds of hay which Sam had left; the water bucket in a corner. She watched as Rod closed both halves of the door, demonstrating how warmly they fitted.

"Your father made a good job of them," she said. It was a generous acknowledgment that Mr. Jennings could do what her father could not.

"Oh, I dunno," Rod said. "Your father helped." Then he slid the bolts, proud of the way they fitted. He doubted that even Arkle had bolts which moved as smoothly. "Got to have good doors, see. Nothing worse than draughts."

Showing off again, Gail thought.

Her mother brought a chair so that she could sit and watch. But Gail didn't want a chair. She sat on a bale of straw, enjoying the sense of sharing. She stayed there until her father went to the field. Then she stood, leaning a shoulder against the wall and listening to the clop of hoofs coming nearer.

Rod ran to the gate. "They're coming."

She watched the corner, surprised by her trembling. It was as though she and Sam were meeting for the first time; but better than that because they already knew each other and had formed a link.

John Fleming led the horse around the corner. They reached the gate which Rod held open. Sam came through boldly, his head inclined toward her father, his feet stepping lightly. Then he saw her. He stopped and stared.

John Fleming leaned on the rope, trying to persuade him forward. But Sam would not come until he was ready. He was waiting for her to speak.

"Come on, Sam," she said.

His ears moved, showing that he was thinking about it. He waited for her to speak again.

"Come on, Sam. You'll catch cold just standing."

He made up his mind. He came forward, his head down and eyes serious. She put up a hand to touch him for the first time. Her hand moved down the long bone of his face.

"My Sam," she said.

Then she put her arms around his neck, leaning on his strength and smelling his warmth. She whispered something which only he was meant to hear. The whispering said, "Better get a move on, Sam. I'm catching up."

CHAPTER TEN

For a while Gail watched her father groom Sam, noticing the routine, always beginning on the neck on the left-hand side; noticing, also, Sam's peculiarities. He didn't like his ears touched. He was ticklish, fidgeting his feet and whisking his tail as soon as the brush came near his chest. When you cleaned his hoofs, he insisted that it be done always in the same order. First the bandaged leg, second the hind on the same side, then the hind on the other side. Conform to this order and he cooperated. Try to change it and he stiffened the leg you wanted, his head as ugly as a mule's.

But after a few weeks Gail became impatient. Watching was not enough. She wanted to do it.

"Not yet," John Fleming said. "You might stumble in the straw. Your leg might give out."

He didn't add that if she stumbled, a frightened thoroughbred might kick her head in. But that was what he meant.

Gail didn't believe it. She didn't argue, but she was resolved to prove him wrong. One Sunday morning the opportunity came.

Mr. Fleming tethered Sam to the staple, but as he began the grooming his wife called from the porch.

"John. The phone."

"Who is it?"

"Alderman Smailes."

John Fleming groaned. Alderman Smailes was a member of the borough council in the market town. He liked publicity; saying anything, promising anything to get his name in the papers. John Fleming came out of the box, guessing that this time Alderman Smailes had a red-hot tip about the council's plan to increase rents or rates. The only condition would be that when the story was printed, the name of Alderman Smailes must be displayed prominently as the watchdog of the ratepayers' interests.

John groaned again as he put the brushes on the shelf. Local councilors came in two kinds: those who were suspicious of publicity, preferring public business to be kept private; and those who tried to use local reporters as personal publicity officers. John wasn't sure which kind he liked least.

"Back in a minute," he said to Gail.

But his wry smile made it plain that it would be much longer than a minute. Alderman Smailes liked the telephone almost as much as he liked publicity.

Gail watched him go. Then she looked at Sam, whose head was half-turned wondering why the grooming had been interrupted. After a while she looked at the brushes on the shelf. She reached for the brushes and moved slowly to the half-door. She looked at Sam and made up her mind. Then she opened the door and went in, moving carefully in the straw.

Sam made a grunting sound, flinching up his head because this was the first time she had entered. He seemed bigger in the box. For a while she stood, waiting for him to become used to her. Then she put up a hand, holding his head collar as she ducked beneath and straightened on the left side.

She held a strap of the head collar with her left hand and brushed his neck with her right. He made small grunting sounds and ground his teeth, resentful that she was continuing what her father had started. He seemed to think that she belonged only at the window during the day and on the outside of the box in morning and evening. She did not belong in here.

She said, "You're silly," and kept the brush moving, refusing to be frightened by the stamping or by the whisking tail. For a while it seemed she was succeeding. Her weight was balanced, so that her left leg was strong enough. Her hand held his head while the brush swept back beyond the wither.

Then it happened. He moved sideways, putting her off balance. The brush blundered to the straw. She grabbed his mane with her right hand, pulling on it as she tried to keep upright. He wrenched from her grasp and brought his head round. Not far but far enough.

The bite was quick. He tried to throw up his head, expecting a blow. But the rope would not let him get away. He fought the rope, leaning backward, his back feet sliding up the straw. His ears were flat. His breathing was furious. For the first time she saw what his strength could do. She was terrified.

She could not get out. She stumbled sideways to the slate shelf, half falling across it as the rope exploded like a gun shot.

He sprang back, his head wild, his nostrils snorting. He pawed his bandaged leg, reaching for her in a long, sweeping movement.

Then she realized. He'd done this before and had probably been beaten across the ears. He was expecting her to beat him. The threatening foreleg was his way of boxing her off.

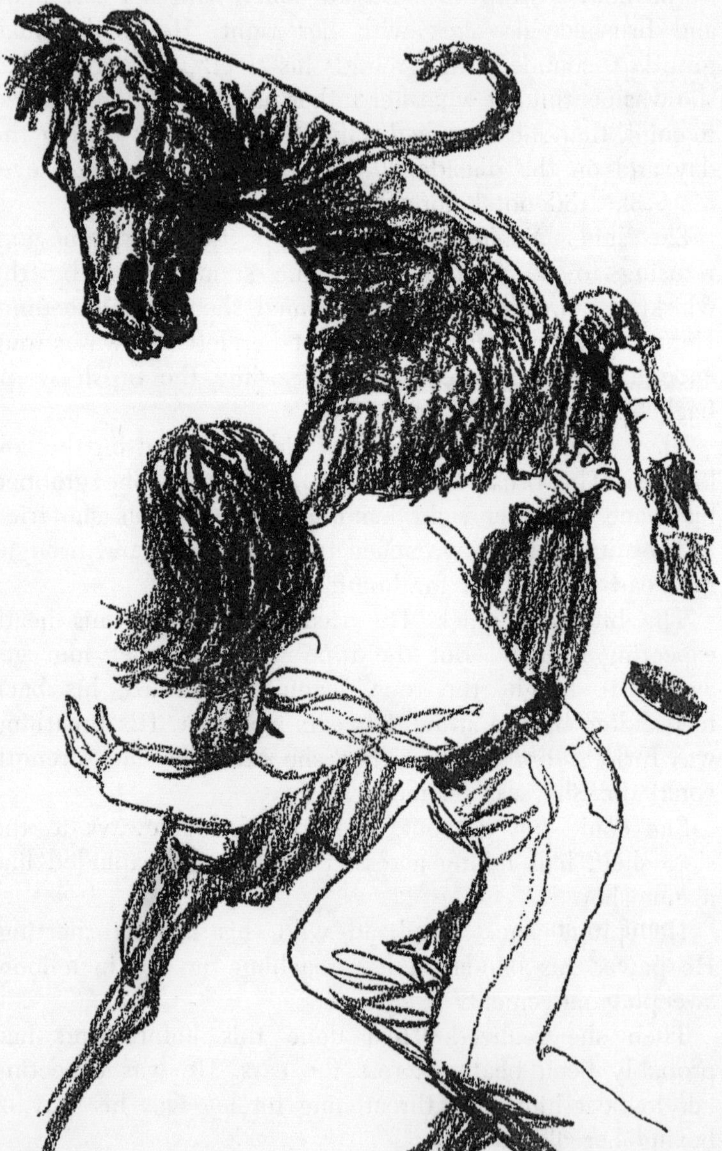

Gail said, "I'm not going to hit you."

Her voice was trembling so that she hardly recognized it. At the same time she admitted the pain in her forearm and clutched it, hugging it against her body. It seemed that she had folded her arms, showing him that she was not going to strike.

Sam looked at her a long time before he was sure. Then his mood changed. The tension went out, so did the fear. He relaxed and brought down his head. He swayed his head from side to side in a bewildered way. She understood what he was trying to say. He was trying to apologize.

"You come to me then," Gail said. "I'm not coming to you."

This wasn't choice, it was necessity. She knew that her left leg would not let her walk toward him. It was trembling, as weak as jelly. She kept assuring him that he must come to her and after what seemed a long time, Sam came. He brushed his forehead against her, the big bone hurting almost as much as his teeth had done. But she understood the difference. There was no malice now. He was using his strength to demonstrate how sorry he was. It wasn't his fault that his head was too hard, his strength too great.

"Steady." Gail wriggled off the shelf. "You're squashing me."

She straightened, still holding the head collar. She meant to stand there, waiting for her father to come back. But Sam's docility encouraged her to do more. She knotted the broken rope and tied it to the staple. Then she crouched for the brush and resumed the grooming. Guilty, she made herself small as her father hurried down the path.

John Fleming looked for her on the bale of straw where

he had left her. Then he stiffened, guessing where she was. He looked sideways above the half door; unable to see his daughter but reassured by Sam. The horse was standing as still as a statue. There was an earnest look in the only eye which John Fleming could see, as though Sam was trying to prove something.

"You shouldn't have gone in." He kept his voice low, speaking to the sounds of brushing on the other side. "Anything might have happened."

Gail didn't answer. She only tugged down the sleeve of her jersey, making sure he didn't see that anything had.

"Let me know when you're tired," John Fleming said.

Gail would not admit that she was tired. She completed the grooming, surprised how long it took and how heavy the brush became.

"Well done," John Fleming said, opening the door for her. Then he added, "You, too," and went in to slap Sam's neck. Sam knew that he could move now. He fretted and stamped, wanting to be out.

Gail waited until she was alone to turn up the sleeve of her jersey and inspect the bruise. It was a beautiful color; blue and green and red. The swelling seemed enormous. She was astonished that one bite could do so much. Not even a bite, she thought. Only a nip.

She wanted to show off such a marvelous bruise, the best she had ever owned and well worth the pain. But it wasn't the sort you could show your parents. She kept it a secret until Rod Jennings came back from the Mission Church.

"Look," she said, turning up her sleeve.

The colors were even deeper. The swelling couldn't have been more spectacular if she'd designed it herself.

"How you get that?"

"Sam," she answered proudly.

Rod looked at it again, his envy showing. "What did you do?"

"Nothing."

"I bet you were scared."

"Wasn't," Gail said. "I just sat there."

"Where?"

"On the slate shelf," Gail said. "I just sat and waited for him to apologize."

It didn't sound true. That was the trouble with truth, Gail thought. She could have invented something much more dramatic.

"Ah," Rod said in disgust. "Trust a girl to get her arm in the way."

Gail hugged it, knowing he was jealous. She hoped the bruise would still be there when she went back to school.

She went back to school after Christmas, taking her desk on the right and filling it with her books as though she'd never been away. The geography class was doing Mediterranean countries. History was the Crusades. The French class was doing verbs. In general science you were safe if you knew about respiration.

She found that because of her mother's encouragement she had kept in touch well enough to earn six out of ten for French verbs and eight for Mediterranean countries; although she received only four for the Crusades because her imagination was stimulated by the name so that she invented instead of sticking to facts.

She was in touch also with school jokes. When a boy pushed in the queue for school dinners she had the right question. "Do you like fish?" She didn't wait for an answer. Jubilantly she added, "Well, there's a nice plaice at the back."

Everyone screamed with laughter, especially those who

had heard it before. The moment of triumph showed how much she owed Rod, for he had told her that this was the new joke and they had giggled together in the stable.

Rod had kept her in touch with nicknames also. The new teacher of maths was Mr. Hole. So his nickname was Minto because of the mint-with-the-hole. She thought that girls invented the best nicknames. Those contrived by boys were always too obscure. Noah, for instance, for Mr. Simpson who taught religious knowledge. Or R.K. Only boys could pronounce that as "Ark" and let their invention jump to "Noah."

She did not even miss hockey and netball as much as she had feared. She missed the honor of being chosen; of staring at her printed name on the team-sheets like a new actress seeing her name in lights. But at the back of her mind was the thought, let them have their team games. I've got Sam.

Sam was in her thoughts so often that when the English teacher let her write an essay on any subject of her choice, she wrote about Sam as though there was nothing else. She wrote too much, too quickly; unable to finish it because there wasn't time, then frightened that Mr. Graves, whose nickname was Skeleton, would not be able to read it. Mr. Graves could not. He wrote "See me" in red ink across it. Then Gail was sure that she was back and that school had not changed at all.

Her life became so crowded that no day was long enough. It began early, because Sam had to be fed and groomed; then the journey across the moor to school in the market town; followed by the journey home and bringing Sam from the field and tea and homework and helping Rod and watching television until her mother said it was time for bed.

She couldn't believe that her world had ever been

confined to one room; that struggling to the spare bedroom had ever been an achievement or that getting down the stairs had ever been a triumph. She felt confident that she could do anything. Well, almost anything.

She told her father, "I'm well enough to ride Sam."

John Fleming smiled, delighted by her confidence yet cautious. He played for time, pretending that no one could ride Sam until Teddy Leech had passed him fit.

"Well, get Teddy over," Gail said. "He'll come at once when he knows how important it is."

Teddy Leech came at the weekend. He unrolled the bandage from Sam's leg and felt the tendons. The leg was still slightly swollen.

"It always will be," Teddy said. "You can't make it new again. But there's nothing there now, not even a twinge."

Gail and Rod crowded closer. Teddy did not say what they wanted to hear, so Rod said, "Is he ready for riding?"

Teddy smiled at their enthusiasm, then looked up to John Fleming. "The sooner the better. He could do with work." Teddy straightened and came from the box. "As long as it's not too far, too fast."

"Let me," Rod said.

John Fleming dared not look at the boy. Nor at his daughter. He wanted to say, it had better be me. Yet he had not ridden for nearly thirty years.

"If it's any help," Teddy said, "I'll come over, ride him in a field. If he's going to play up, it'll be the first time."

Almost John agreed, recognizing the good sense and appreciating the offer. But he understood better than anyone the part which the horse had played in Gail's recovery. All her striving had been toward him; all the striving had had this as a natural climax.

He said, "It has to be Gail."

Teddy gave him a long look. "You realize what you're risking?"

In a flash of fright John saw the horse rearing, his daughter falling. If that happened he would never forgive himself. Yet if he refused . . . He looked at Gail, trusting the link which had developed between her and Sam and which made their relationship unique. He darted her a pale smile, then reached for the saddle.

The girths were of nylon, the bridle had a rubber bit. Sam played with the bit, listening to the chime of the snaffle rings. He was more impatient than ever to get out.

"I brought this leading tape." Teddy clipped it to one ring and slipped it through the other. "Either you or me walking at his head all the time. That's risk enough."

"I'll do it," John Fleming said.

He led Sam from the box, leaning to make him stand. Then he nodded to Gail and in the instant of moving forward, she almost changed her mind. Sam seemed huge. One buck could loosen the grip of her knees, a second could have her down and broken. Almost she said, "Let somebody else." But Rod was watching, wanting her to refuse so that he could be the first.

She walked toward Sam, letting him see her and understand that it would be her weight on his back. She rubbed his face and patted his neck. Then she nodded to Teddy Leech. He crouched, his hands forming a step for her foot. She put in her left foot and he straightened, lifting her up and up, incredibly high, like a circus acrobat. She widened her legs for the saddle.

Sam started, dragging her father in a circle. She took the reins as each foot groped for its stirrup. Over a shoulder she was aware of her mother's white face, with Rod looking up. She heard Teddy call a warning to grip with her knees. Then Sam was moving out of the yard with her father at his head.

For a while Sam danced, not sure what was expected of him and showing his willingness to gallop. Then he settled to a walk, which was all they seemed to want. He walked away from Gorse Blossom and up the hill, his head high and interested because he had not gone this way before.

John Fleming led him to a grass path between the road and the moorland wall. Its grass had been bitten short by sheep and ponies. Imprints of their hoofs were in the mud. Sam looked down at the imprints, placing his big feet carefully as though he would not step in the imprints of common animals. They moved quietly up the hill and John was deceived by the quietness. He relaxed, looking backward to his daughter and at that moment the car appeared.

It was not traveling fast but its roar was sudden. Sam jumped and lurched sideways. John tried to hang on, but his feet were too slow. He stumbled and the tape slipped. Suddenly he was down and Sam was free with the car squealing its brakes in a desperate attempt to stop.

Sam crossed the road in front of it. One bound took him up the grass slope on the other side. But he was too close to the wall to jump it. Gail brought his head around, an instinctive tightening of her right hand because she was terrified of galloping downhill.

She turned up the hill, standing in the stirrups as Sam fought for his head. She had a confused picture of Sam's mane in her face, of his ears pricked, of his angry breathing. Her knees could feel the thumping of his heart. Mixed up in this picture was the car, drawn to one side

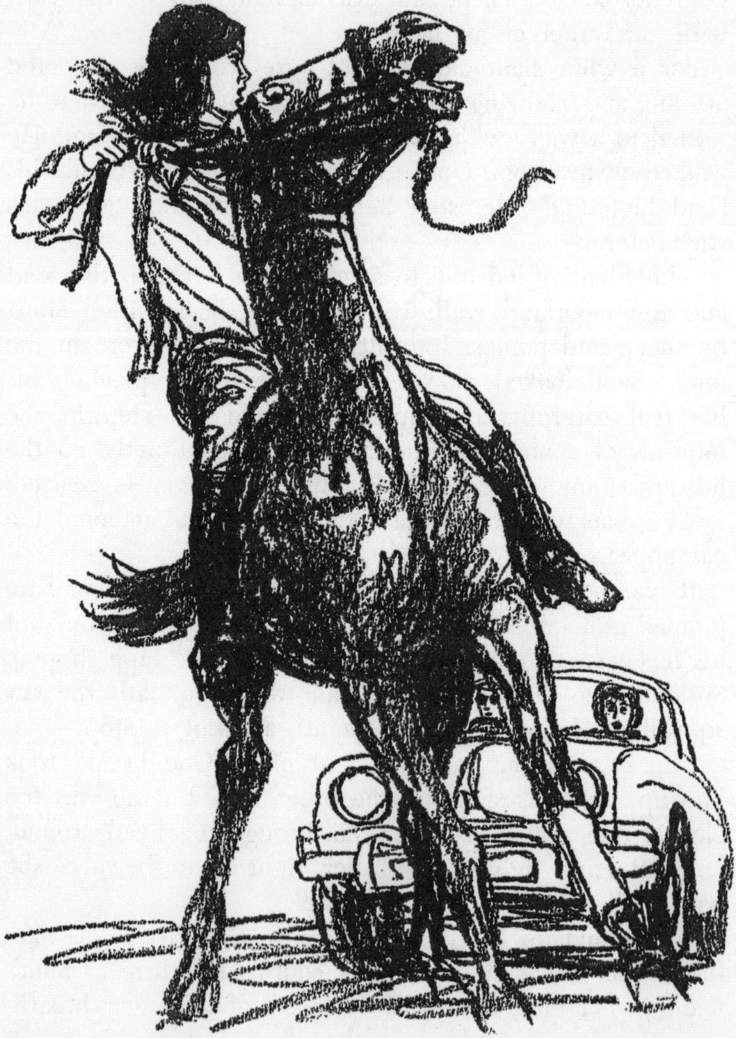

of the road with a frightened face at the window; then her father, scrambling up and running.

Sam hammered up the hill and the wind in her face had a strange smell. It was the smell of sweat. White flecks were splashes of it. For a while his power seemed inexorable. Then she felt the pounding going out of his hind-quarters. The rhythm of his shoulders changed as his stride shortened. He was getting tired. Or perhaps he had forgotten what had startled him. She called to him, begging her arms to be strong enough. Sam gave in as they reached the top of the hill.

He stopped, his snorting pretending that he could have gone on for ever. White froth dripped from his bit as he chimed the rings. His smell was like wet coats when you dry them before a fire. He threw up his head as Gail leaned to pat his neck. Now he was contemptuous of the car, scarcely bothering to glance at it. He wanted only to go home.

Gail turned him down the path which the moorland animals had made. Teddy Leech and her mother were at the gate; Rod was running up the lower slope. Gail waved, assuring them that it was all right. She saw her father in the middle of the road, his hair seeming thinner than ever as it shredded in the wind. Then she recognized the man who stood beside the car.

Dr. Craig, why's he here?

But Sam gave her no time to think about it; only to feel a glow of pride because it seemed appropriate that Dr. Craig, who had pressed her to do so much, should see her doing more than he had ever asked.

The doctor and her father walked near her down the hill. Mrs. Fleming and Teddy Leech came up to meet them, but none walked nearer than Rod. They were smiling, laughing, their voices a muddle of excitement and relief. Sam responded, lilting like a champion.

It seemed that Gail had won something. Not a race, for Sam would never win another race. But something.

CHAPTER ELEVEN

Spring came late to Dartmoor, calling new colors out of winter grayness. The lengthening days gave Gail more time with Sam and each evening she rode up the hill and along the skyline.

At first she timed the ride to be about an hour; forty minutes out and twenty back because that was how Sam pulled when he realized he was going home. But the rides grew longer as his leg became stronger. They rambled across the heather and up the bracken hills, fording streams and jumping gullies, exploring corners of the moor which she had not found before.

She was miles from Gorse Blossom that Thursday evening when she saw a black car on the hill. She watched it crawl across the shoulder of the moor. It stopped at the crossroads and men in uniforms got out. One moved to the middle of the road, holding up a hand to an approaching lorry.

The lorry stopped. One policeman talked with the driver while the other moved to the back, clambering to peer over the tailboard. Their search was brief. Then they stood back and the lorry moved on. Simultaneously the policemen saw her and waved. She waved back. Only when they waved again did she realize that they were beckoning.

"Come on, Sam," she said.

Sam put down his head and cantered across the heather toward the crossroads.

"Barbara," John Fleming called, closing the door.

His wife answered from the room at the end of the passage. "Won't be a minute." She appeared in the doorway. "You're nice and early."

John took off his coat and as he hung it on a peg, the telephone rang. He groaned, guessing it was for him.

"I'll get it." Mrs. Fleming's heels tip-tapped along the stone-flagged passage until she reached the carpet of the hall. "Let's hope it isn't somebody calling you out."

She picked up the phone, putting on her special telephone voice. She always put it on when she didn't know who was at the other end. If it was a stranger, she kept it on throughout the conversation. But if it was relative or friend, she relaxed into her normal voice.

"Hullo, Moorhampton two-six."

Then she listened and said "Yes" twice; the second time doubtfully, looking at her husband to make sure that he wanted to be "in." Then she held out the phone.

The policemen watched the girl riding toward them. One said, "Know who it is?" And the other answered, "John Fleming's daughter. She's always riding round this time of day."

They watched the horse splash through a stream and bound up the bank on the other side. "Nice horse," the first policeman said.

They parted as Sam came up to them. Each put a hand on the bridle, restraining his impatience as they looked up to Gail. She recognized one of them; Patrol Constable Lewis, a friend of her father.

"Where you been riding?"

Gail waved a hand toward the northern hills.

"Seen anybody?"

"No," Gail said. "Not a thing."

"You know what's happened, don't you? What we're here for?"

"I can guess," Gail said.

"A prisoner escaped," Constable Lewis said. "Broke from a working party about four o'clock. He might be anywhere, so keep your eyes skinned."

"All right," Gail said.

"And take a straight line home," Constable Lewis added. "Soon be dark anyway."

They watched Gail canter away. She was standing in the stirrups, leaning forward as Sam pulled for home. The first policeman said, "I suppose she'll be all right." And Constable Lewis answered, "She's safe enough. Nobody could catch her on that horse."

John Fleming put down the phone and reached for his coat. "Another break-out."

"Surely you've got time for a cup." Mrs. Fleming came from the living room. "I've got the kettle on."

He fumbled the buttons. "Been out since four o'clock and no one's seen a sign."

She knew that he wouldn't listen to protests about you must eat, surely there's time for a cup of tea. She put the scarf around his neck. She'd given it to him last Christmas, but he never wore it unless she remembered.

"Prisoner called Hennessy, doing seven years for armed robbery." He groped in a pocket, making sure that he had the car keys. "But it doesn't seem a planned break-out. He just made a dash from a quarry party."

"Well, take care." She followed him to the door. "And

keep in touch. If you're going to be a long time, keep in touch by telephone."

John Fleming was on the porch before he remembered. "Where's Gail?"

"Riding." Mrs. Fleming looked up the hill. "Went over an hour ago. I told her not to be so long."

John hesitated, watching the hill. When he spoke he was not talking to his wife. He was talking to himself, reassuring himself. "She'll probably see one of the roadblocks. She'll see the police and guess what's happened and come straight home."

Yet he did not go to the car. His imagination was flashing pictures of what might happen.

"She'll be all right," Mrs. Fleming said. "Gail knows how dangerous it is and no one could get near as long as she's got Sam."

He darted a glance, realizing that it was true. He was moving toward the car as the phone shrilled. Over a shoulder he said, "If that's another London paper, tell them I'm on my way."

Mrs. Fleming watched him go, then went in to the telephone. "Yes," she told the urgent voice at the other end, "he's on his way. He'll be ringing you as soon as he can."

Then she went back to the porch, watching the hill and wondering if those London newspapers realized the dangers. Living within seven miles of the most formidable prison in Britain. That strained the nerves of people in lonely houses in a way which no London newspaper could understand.

Especially my nerves, Barbara Fleming thought. I've never got used to it.

There was movement on the hill. Sheep which had been as still as white stones were moving down the slope.

She knew that something had disturbed them, for sheep would not willingly come down hill so near darkness. Their instinct was to find high ground at night.

For a moment she was frightened, because perhaps the sheep had been startled by a man. Perhaps the man was running, crouched low in the manner of a fugitive. Then a blurred shape came out of the twilight and she recognized it with relief.

She was at the gate as Gail rode down the hill. She didn't need to ask if her daughter knew what had happened. The sweat on Sam's chest was enough. She began to say, "You've been riding too fast," but that wouldn't be fair. She'd wanted her daughter to come quickly.

"Like the wind," Gail said breathlessly. "He's never pulled so hard."

Mrs. Fleming put a hand on the bridle, looking up at Sam's fretful ears, at his sharp, mistrustful look around. He seemed suspicious, and she wondered if he had sensed some menace on the moor. She slapped his neck, applauding his intelligence, but the slapping was a distraction and Sam butted away her hand. He was breathing heavily, staring toward the dark trees near the house.

"He wants to go in." Gail slipped down. "It'll take an hour to get him dry."

But Mrs. Fleming did not take her eyes from Sam. It seemed that his suspicions were telling her something which she only half understood. She looked where he was staring; at the blackness beneath the tall spruce which provided a windbreak for the house. She thought, it's nothing. Yet even as she decided this, she heard herself say, "I'll stay with you."

Gail led Sam to his box, and Mrs. Fleming stayed near during the long process of drying and cleaning and feeding. Meanwhile darkness crept down the hill like a silent army, stalking closer and closer until it occupied the yard. She looked over her shoulder to the trees, rebuking herself because it was foolish to be frightened yet impatient for Gail to finish.

"Come on, it's getting cold."

She was fretting to get back to the house, as though only in the house could they be safe. She hustled Gail within, then lowered the iron bar across the door. It was safer than any lock. A burglar might pick a lock, but he could not break an iron bar.

The bar gave her a feeling of security. Two logs on the fire encouraged a blaze which cheered her spirit. She began to mock the fears in her head, aware that Gail was watching and that she must make this evening seem the same as any other.

"Your meal's in the oven. You need something hot after riding so far."

Then she switched on the television. She tried to watch, to be amused as she made sure that Gail ate enough, but the television comedians seemed to be living in another world.

The only world which mattered was here; this room, with darkness pressing at the windows and black silence all the way to the sky. She scarcely heard Gail's questions. When will Daddy be back? How much will he be paid for working tonight? Will it be in all the papers tomorrow? Mrs. Fleming didn't want to talk. She wanted to listen. She turned down the television, straining to hear without realizing what she was listening for.

Once she thought she heard something, and looked toward the passage and the brown door at the end of it.

"What's the matter?" Gail asked.

"Hush." Mrs. Fleming listened again, but of course

there was nothing. She tried to laugh. "I thought I heard something."

"What?"

Mrs. Fleming saw surprise in her daughter's eyes. The surprise was about to become fright. Desperately she said, "Well, Rod, perhaps. Coming for help with his homework."

Gail seemed to be half convinced, so Mrs. Fleming added, "You know what Rod's like on Thursday nights. One look at his geometry book and he's here like a shot."

She cleared an end of the table, making space for homework books. She waited until Gail had moved from one chair to another. Then she carried the dishes to the kitchen, not closing the door between. It seemed to be an ordinary evening; her daughter's head bowed over a map of the Mediterranean, the fire blazing and dishes in the sink. What could be more ordinary? Yet something was wrong.

She stood in the kitchen, all her senses straining to pick up what was wrong. It seemed that the old house was tense; as tense and suspicious as Sam had been in the yard. She thought, somebody's moving outside. Somebody's trying to get in.

"Where're you off then?" Mrs. Jennings asked.

Rod zipped his weatherproof jacket. Its chest bulged, showing where he had stuffed his geometry. "Over Windy's," he said at the door.

"Well, you watch out then. You heard the six o'clock news. They haven't caught him yet."

But Mrs. Jennings was not really alarmed. She'd lived all her life on the moor; had grown accustomed to alarms and wild rumors when prisoners escaped. She liked to make a joke of the dangers, pretending that if a prisoner dared to break into her house, she'd "give him one with me umbrella, he'd be glad to go back after I'd finished with him."

Rod closed the door. There was a torch in his pocket, but he did not need it. He knew the path to the stream like daylight; then along the bank to the tall trees of Gorse Blossom. Lighted windows were showing through the trees. One was the kitchen, the other the living room. They told him that he need not hurry. Gail hadn't gone to bed yet, so Minto wouldn't be writing "See me" in the morning.

Rod hadn't a care in the world until he reached the stone wall. Then he stopped, listening, not sure what he had heard but sure that he had heard something. On the other side of the wall were the trees. Twenty yards along was the gate. His first instinct was to duck below the level of the wall. His second was to run home, risking nought out of ten and the worst that Minto could do.

Then he took his fright by the scruff of the neck and talked to it severely. What would Wyatt Earp have done? Wyatt wouldn't have legged it for home, would he? Wyatt Earp would have investigated, that's what.

Rod crouched a long time, wondering what there was to investigate and why fate should pick on him. He listened again but could hear nothing. He straightened slowly, peering over the wall but seeing nothing. Then he moved along the wall to the gate, beginning to believe that he had been mistaken. Some trick of the imagination. Only a clot would stay here, playing games with shadows.

Rod waited a long time at the gate, afraid to lift the hasp because the gate was old and stiff and would whine as it moved. To climb would be safer; but not here, where anyone watching the gate would see his black shape coming over. To move along, into the shadow of the barn, that would be good sense.

He crept into the shadow of the barn, feeling that Wyatt Earp would have approved because only tenderfoots took unnecessary risks. He found a place to climb and put a foot into the first hole and scrambled up and waited, surprised by his panting, by the hammering of his heart. Anyone in the darkness would surely hear him. That same anyone would know he was terrified.

Rod tried to control his breathing. He crouched on the top of the wall, listening to nothing; only the steady sounds of Sam, eating hay in the box. He listened so long that he began to mock himself. What am I doing crouching on the wall? I'd look a right nit if the door opened and Mrs. Fleming shone a torch and said, "Rod, whatever are you doing on the wall?" What could I answer to that? Picking wall flowers?

Self-scorn drove him over the wall. He dropped quietly and in that instant something changed. Something which had been there so steadily that he had ceased to hear it was taken away. He crouched, wondering what it was. Then he realized. The sounds of Sam eating hay; they had stopped. Sam had heard him.

He smiled because Sam hearing him, that was nothing. But as he straightened he saw something else. Something moved across the window light. It was as quick as a bat and as silent. His eyes pierced the darkness, trying to see where the quick shadow had gone. For a while he couldn't find it. Then his listening picked up a slight sound and he saw a movement, darker than the night, near a corner of the house. The slight sound was repeated. Rod imagined he could hear breathing as frightened as his own.

He looked around for a place to hide. He saw the darkness of the barn and darted toward it, needing to be near something familiar and trusting Sam to protect him. He knew that Sam was tense with listening.

Rod crouched near the door of the box, staring up the slope toward the house. Now he could hear nothing, could not see the dark movement. He guessed that whoever it was had moved toward the back of the house; to the small furtive door which Quakers had used when they had needed to meet in secret. He waited, wondering what would happen and what he should do.

Gail looked at the clock. "Well, where is he then?"

Mrs. Fleming didn't answer. She was packing homework books into the satchel, as though by hastening Gail to bed she could push evening into night and hasten the return of her husband.

"You said yourself," Gail said. "Rod always comes on a Thursday. So there must be something wrong."

Mrs. Fleming placed the satchel behind an armchair. "Perhaps he can do it himself for once."

"Hah," Gail said.

"All right. As soon as you're in the bathroom, I'll ring his mother. Ask if he's ill or something."

Gail settled for that. She went up the stairs to the bedtime ritual of hot water, scented soap, toothbrush and toothpaste and the taste of peppermint. Mrs. Fleming waited for the sounds of brushing. Then she called, "I'm ringing now."

She dialed the Jennings' number and held the telephone to an ear. Nothing happened. She could not hear the burring noise which would be the bell ringing at the other end. She dialed again. Then she put down the phone and stared at it, beginning to guess what had happened.

"What's the matter?" Gail called. "I thought you were going to ask."

Mrs. Fleming started, almost blurting the truth. Then

she answered, "Number engaged," and picked up the phone and dialed again. After a while she said, "Mrs. Jennings? This is Barbara Fleming. We were expecting Rod . . ." She talked to herself, pretending that Mrs. Jennings was explaining Rod's absence. He'd been excused geometry for tonight. The maths teacher had forgotten to set any.

"What?" Gail cried from her bedroom. "Minto set some for me."

"It's true," Mrs. Fleming said. Then she added, "Well, thank you, Mrs. Jennings. As long as everything's all right."

"Old Minto never lets me off," Gail wailed. "He always sets girls plenty."

Mrs. Fleming put down the phone. There were no doubts now in her head. Someone was outside and the wires had been cut. She was alone with her daughter and whoever was in the darkness.

She straightened, refusing to give in to her fright. She went up the stairs, compelling herself to act a part as though it was an ordinary bedtime. She tucked in the covers, kissed Gail good-night and switched off the bedroom light. But the light on the landing remained because that had been the custom since early childhood. In the doorway she said, "I'll be downstairs."

"Good-night, Mummy."

Mrs. Fleming hesitated, listening to what might be waiting in the passage. Then she said, "Good-night, Gail" and went down to the bottom step. There she hesitated a long time, afraid to look along the passage.

The passage was empty. She stared at the brown door at the end, where the dairy had been when Gorse Blossom had been a farm. It seemed that the door had been open a crack, that it was gently closing as she looked at it.

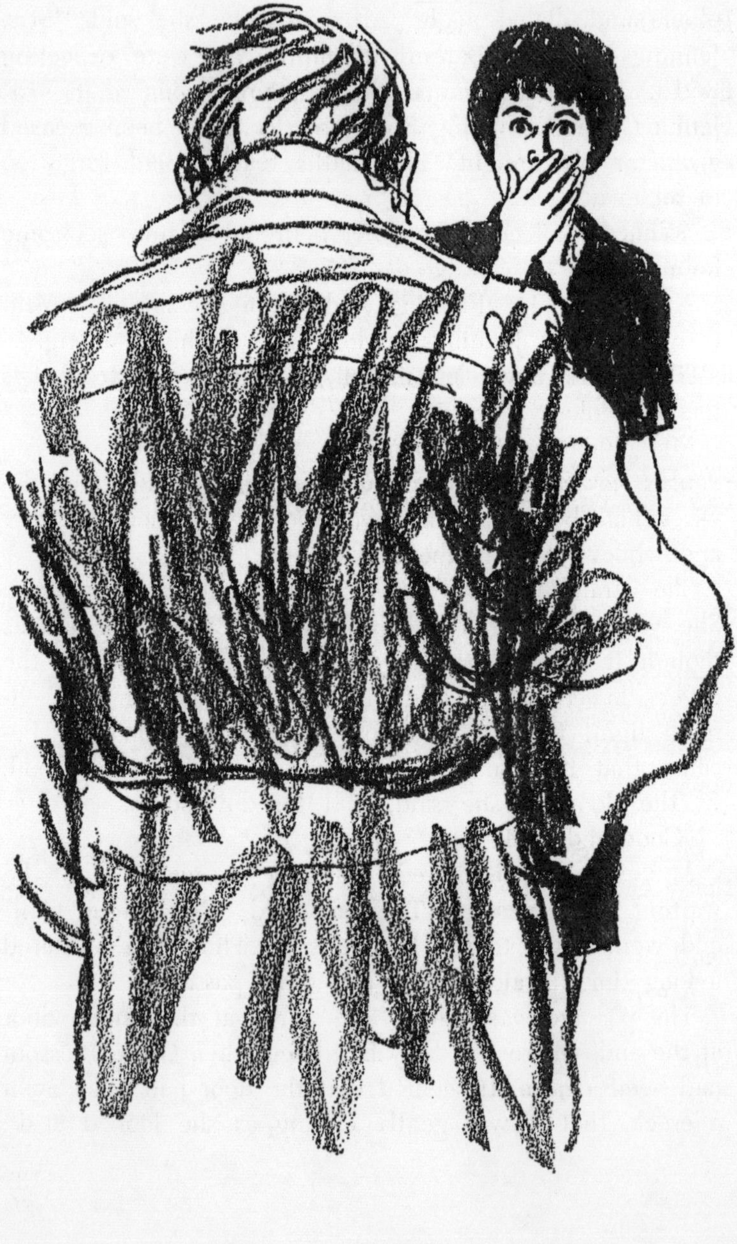

Her terror tried to deny it. No, no, it can't be. But she knew the man was there.

She ran to the living room because it had lights and a fire and because lights and a fire made it seem safer. She watched the doorway, sensing rather than hearing him come from the room which had been the dairy. He was creeping along the passage. It seemed that she heard his stillness.

She was waiting for him, yet when he appeared her gasp was like surprise. He wore a coat over his prison uniform. His eyes were black and quick, probing the corners of the room, making sure that she was alone. Then he came in, his hands in the pockets of his coat.

She could not believe that this was Hennessy, a convicted thug. He looked ordinary, thin and small and cold. She heard herself say, "What do you want?"

"You alone?"

The question was sudden, his glance was as sharp as a thrust. It told her that he had only just broken in; that from the room at the end of the passage he had not heard her talking to Gail or pretending to telephone.

"My husband will be back any minute."

Hennessy smiled, not believing it. He glanced to the opened door of the kitchen. "Food. Clothes. Do what I say and there's nothing to be frightened of."

Mrs. Fleming thought, I'm not frightened. That's the funny thing. Not half as frightened as I was before the phone was cut. She straightened, looking at him defiantly.

"You'll never get away with it."

CHAPTER TWELVE

Gail opened her eyes. The voice in the dark room said, "You'll never get away with it." It was eerie, like Joan of Arc hearing voices in the air. She recognized her mother's voice, although the interroom link always distorted it. She lifted her head from the pillow, listening intently, hearing faint sounds from the kitchen, then a man's voice, dark and menacing.

"I told you. Do as I say and you'll be all right."

Her mother answered from the kitchen, "I'm doing it as fast as I can."

Gail sat up, remembering the policemen on the moor, and guessing who the man was. Her first instinct was to shout, to protect her mother, as though shouting could frighten the man and make him run.

But shouting could be no use. She lifted back the covers and crept out, reaching for sweater and jodhpurs. An idea began to form in her head. If she could get out of the house. If she could reach the police at the crossroads. But how to get out and how to reach them?

The passage, she thought. Down the stairs and along the passage to the door which the Quakers had used. She had no riding boots in her bedroom, so she moved to the landing in her socks. She listened. Her mother had come from the kitchen, bringing him food. Presumably he was eating what he could and stuffing the rest into a pocket. That meant he was occupied, less likely to hear a sound on the stairs.

The stairs behaved themselves as she went down. They didn't make a sound, showing that the old house was on her side. The door to the living room was ajar. She listened tensely. Her mother was pouring something, giving the man a hot drink. She allowed her mother time to pass the cup. Then she darted from the stairs to the passage and along it to the brown door, fighting the temptation to run.

She passed through the room which had been the dairy, opened the back door, waited a second and slipped out, her feet wincing from loose stones. The darkness was blinding. She groped around the corner of the house and found the path to the yard. Over her right shoulder the curtained window of the living room looked warm and innocent. It gave no hint of what was happening within.

She moved down to the yard, her socks making no sound. She reached the darkness of the barn and ducked into it, putting out a hand for the bolt of Sam's box. She touched somebody. She opened her mouth to scream and a hand covered it. Instinctively she bit and the hand flinched away.

"Hey," Rod said in her ear.

Mrs. Fleming watched Hennessy eat, knowing what he would demand as soon as his hunger was satisfied. He would demand clothes because not until he discarded his prison uniform would he have even a slim chance of reaching Plymouth.

She thought, I'll give them to him. I'll fetch an old suit of John's, fetching it myself so he won't go up the stairs and find Gail. She knew that a brave woman would refuse, would somehow outsmart him. But she was not a brave woman. She had no clever ruses in her head. Her one idea was to protect Gail. As long as he doesn't find Gail, she thought.

But when he finished the food, he would not let her go up alone. Perhaps he thought she would signal from a window, although as far as she knew there was no one on the moor to see a signal. He followed so closely that she heard his breathing, smelled his breath. They reached the landing. On the right was the door to Gail's room. It was opened. The landing light made a wedge of yellow that touched Gail's bed.

Mrs. Fleming hurried past it, hoping he would not look in. But Hennessy pushed the door wider, looking in to the bed. Mrs. Fleming expected to hear Gail scream. She turned wildly, ready to protect her daughter, to scratch his eyes if he threatened Gail.

The bed was empty.

She stared at it stupidly, more dumbfounded than Hennessy seemed to be. She knew her surprise was a giveaway and said the first thing which came into her head.

"My daughter . . . out . . . went out hours ago."

Hennessy's eyes didn't believe it.

"Out with her father. That's why I'm not worried." Mrs. Fleming tried to laugh. It sounded terrible. "I'd be worried, of course, if she was out on her own."

But the bed was not made. There was the imprint of a head in the pillow. That had to be explained, so she hurried into the room, complaining that Gail was always untidy. "I tell her to make her bed each morning, but she never does."

Hennessy knew there was something wrong, but he thought she was playing for time.

"Leave it."

He beckoned and Mrs. Fleming came out.

"The clothes," Hennessy said.

Mrs. Fleming passed into the big bedroom, opening a wardrobe and removing a hanger. She threw a suit on the bed, still talking about Gail and how untidy children were these days. But behind the talk her thoughts were racing, wondering how much Gail had heard and where she was hiding.

"I can't see," Gail whispered.

Rod took the torch from his pocket, holding his hand over the glass to shield the beam. A pink light filtered between his fingers. It was enough for Gail to find Sam's head and put the reins over.

"Get a move on," Rod whispered.

"Hold the light steady then." Gail slipped the bridle over Sam's ears. "He doesn't like being disturbed in the dark. He knows there's something wrong."

"Sssssh," Rod said. That was the trouble with girls. They talked too much.

"Ssssh yourself," Gail whispered. "Take that straw, put it in the yard, all the way to the gate."

"What for?"

"Now who's wasting time?"

Rod lifted wedges of straw in his arms and scattered them, making a path to the gate. The rustle seemed loud. He glanced to the house, startled by the sudden switch on of a light.

"There's a light upstairs," he whispered.

Gail led out Sam, leaning into him, compelling him to walk along the straw. They reached the gate as Rod opened it. She held back her left leg and he tried to lift her, surprised by her weight. She was still hanging as

Sam fretted away. She clung, wriggling up and getting her right leg over.

"You forgot something," Rod whispered. "You got no shoes on."

Gail didn't hear. She guided Sam to the grass track which climbed the hill. He threw his head, anxious to get this over, whatever it was. But she knew how dangerous the track could be in darkness. The turf was uneven. There were sudden dips and rises. She crouched low, staring at the ground, trying to see the depressions before he reached them.

Rod listened to the hoofs, astonished that no one in the house had heard. He waited until the light in the upper window went out. Then he ran beside the wall toward the stream and beyond it to his home.

Of course his mother didn't believe him. She cried, "You been playing games again." But his excitement, his panting seemed to be genuine.

"I told you," Rod said. "I seen him cut the wires."

Mrs. Jennings shot another look because you could never tell. Boys played such weird games; Freddie Winter one minute, Destry Rides Again the next. You never knew where you were. But this time it might be different . . .

She lifted the telephone, dialing the Flemings' number. No answer. Not even a burring sound.

"I told you," Rod said. "He cut the wires before he broke in."

Then Mrs. Jennings hurried. She dialed a number three times, very quickly. "Police," she said, her voice shaking. When a man's voice answered from the police station at the market town, she said in a frightened gabble, "Gorse Blossom, the convict's there, in the house and Mrs. Fleming alone, frightened out of her wits."

Gail saw the lights of the police cars long before she reached them. The lights of other cars stopped briefly at the crossroads, then moved on, seeming to move without sound because she was too far away to hear their engines. She could hear only Sam's breathing, the pounding of his hoofs, his grunting as he encountered a sudden rise.

She wanted to shout, but she knew the police could not see a black shape galloping in the dark. She was almost on them before they saw her. Then their astonishment showed in their faces. Patrol Constable Lewis moved quickly to hold the bridle. White splashes flecked his uniform as Sam shook his head.

"Home," Gail panted. "My mother."

Another uniform crossed the yellow headlamps. He wore the peaked cap of an inspector. "What's this?"

"John Fleming's daughter, sir," Constable Lewis said. "Looks as though she's had a fright."

"Not me." Gail leaned down, her breath like smoke on the night air. "My mother, alone with him. He broke in . . ."

"Where?" the inspector snapped.

"Gorse Blossom, sir," Lewis answered.

"You know it?"

"Yes, sir. Along the side road from the fork."

"Right then."

Boots were running. Doors opened and slammed. One of the black cars backed a little and prepared to swing away.

"Wait," the inspector snapped. "Take one of the dogs."

Gail saw an alsatian cross the headlights, pulling on its leash. It got into the back, and its handler followed. The car roared toward the fork. The inspector sat in the front seat of another car, speaking on the radio; giving instructions to other cars in the vicinity.

Gail turned away, with no plan in her head except to reach home as quickly as possible and dash into the house and make sure that her mother was all right. Sam wanted home, also. His stride lengthened, expressing his yearning for the only place in the world which mattered. They climbed the slight rise which had seemed so steep and dangerous when they had gone down. On the left were the lights of the police car. Then the lights of another appeared.

At first Gail thought they were the lights of a second police car, but as it drew nearer, overtaking her as she rode beside the road, she threw back a glance and recognized that striving engine, that shabby radiator.

The car slowed as it came alongside. Her father's face was at the window. It was white and frightened. His hand signaled her to stop, but Sam could not be stopped so easily. She had to stand in the stirrups, fighting his head. Not until they were near the hill which looked down to Gorse Blossom did he slow to a trot, then to a walk. Even then he would not stand. He fretted in a circle as her father got out.

"Gail, what are you doing?"

She couldn't explain. She called, "Somebody had to. The police were miles away." Then she wondered, how did you know?

"I tried to phone," John Fleming said. "Guessed there must be something when the line was dead."

The police car was stopped at the top of the hill. Its lights were extinguished. Doors opened and closed quietly as the men got out, looking down to the only window which was lit. The living room window. All else was dark and silent.

Lewis said, "No telling if he's still there."

"If he ever was," another constable answered. "You know what people are for rumors."

"That girl wouldn't make a mistake," Lewis said. "He was there right enough. Might still be."

His companion grumbled, "In which case he'll take some cornering."

Lewis leaned into the car and spoke on its radio. After a while he straightened and turned to John Fleming.

"We're waiting here. Other cars coming."

"But you can't wait." John looked to the window. "My wife's there."

"He won't hurt her, John. He'll just grab food, clothes and cash and off."

"You can't be sure."

"That's the way it usually is. But he's got no chance now. So wait a while, John." Lewis glanced up to Gail. "And you. Get off that horse. Don't you dare go near till we say."

Gail got down, patting Sam and persuading him to be patient. He dropped his head to the grass. It was thin moorland grass, but it would have to do. He snatched quick, petulant bites. She looked to her father as he slipped behind the wheel of his car.

"Look, I'm going down."

"You dare," Lewis said.

"I'm going," John Fleming said. "If he's there, I'll flush him out."

"Hennessy's dangerous."

"He needn't know the police are anywhere near. It'll be as though I'm just coming home in the usual way." John Fleming let in the clutch. "I'm going, Lewis. Don't try to stop me."

Lewis tried to stop him, then stumbled backward as

148

the car roared over the edge of the hill. It went down, its lights blazing. It seemed that John Fleming was making as much noise, as much light as he could, informing the house that he was coming.

Hennessy stepped quickly to the window, lifting an edge of the curtain. "One car, coming fast."

Mrs. Fleming took an involuntary step, but Hennessy dropped the curtain and flattened against the wall. His right hand came from his pocket. There was a knife in it. The knife had been honed and sharpened until its blade was as long and thin as a dagger.

"Who is it?"

"I don't know," Barbara Fleming answered. "How can I if I can't see?"

"Listen." Hennessy's lips were thin, his eyes were flicking. Now he was dangerous, looking for an excuse to use the knife. "If it's yours, you'll recognize the engine."

Barbara Fleming had already recognized it. "It's my husband coming."

"Is he alone?"

"Yes."

"How can you be sure?"

"He always is."

"You said just now . . . your daughter. You said they were out together."

Mrs. Fleming saw the mistake and tried to put it right. But Hennessy was beside her in two strides, his hand on her wrist and twisting. "Where's your daughter then? Where's she hiding then?"

Mrs. Fleming shook her head, her distress making it plain that truly she didn't know. They listened. The sounds of the car were coming through the gate. She saw Hennessy's right hand tighten on the knife.

"Don't you dare. My husband's a kind man. Don't you dare hurt him."

Hennessy's mouth thinned in what might have been a smile. "That depends . . . on you as well as him."

The car came through the gate and stopped near the garage. Hennessy waited for the sounds of it being backed, of garage doors being closed. There were none.

"He's not putting it away."

"He never does," Barbara Fleming said. "Not when he has to go out again."

They heard a door slam, then footsteps on the slope.

"I tell you what to do." Hennessy's whisper was urgent. "You let him come in, without a sign anything's wrong."

"What are you going to do?"

"Neither of you will get hurt. If I get what I want."

Hennessy moved to the wall, flattening his back against it. He held the knife in his right hand, shooting a warning to Mrs. Fleming as footsteps reached the porch.

The door opened and John Fleming came into the hall. His hat was on the back of his head, his scarf was dangling, the buttons of his coat were unfastened. He looked at his wife in the doorway of the living room. He smiled as he sighed, showing her that he was tired and glad to be home.

"Cold. It'll be nice to see a fire." He hung up his coat, rubbing his hands as he turned toward her. "Well, how's it been? All right?"

"Yes," Barbara Fleming answered. "Quite all right."

"And Gail, what about Gail?"

"All right," she said.

The conversation was strange, as stiff as the conversation in a bad play.

"They haven't found Hennessy yet. Miles away by now.

Someone was supposed to have seen him near Moretonhampstead. That means he's aiming for Exeter."

John put his hand on her arm. They crossed the threshold of the living room and Hennessy slammed the door.

"Turn around," Hennessy said.

They turned around. Hennessy was smiling, crouching slightly. His knife was moving, inviting John Fleming to attack.

For a moment Barbara thought her husband might. She saw the darkening of his eyes, the quick flush of anger. It was the anger of a man whose home has been invaded, whose wife and daughter have been frightened. John Fleming was seldom angry, but she knew that anger could make him as dangerous in his way as Hennessy was in another. She clutched his arm, warning him what a knife could do.

John Fleming did not move. He regarded Hennessy a long moment, then laughed. The suit didn't fit.

"You can cut that out." Laughter made Hennessy nervous. Then he remembered what John had said in the hall. "Moretonhampstead, is that where they're looking?" Hennessy seemed amused, his vanity pleased by the stupidity of the police. "Well, that gives me a fair chance." He held out his left hand, the forefinger beckoning. "Come on, you know what I want."

John Fleming groped in a pocket and brought out his car keys. He tossed them and Hennessy caught them.

"How much petrol?"

"Almost three gallons." It seemed that John was making it easy, almost offering his car for an easy get-away. "I filled up earlier."

Hennessy nodded. "One other thing. Money."

Again John Fleming did not hesitate. He put a hand

into an inner pocket and brought out three crumpled notes; two pounds and ten shillings.

"This all you got?"

"It's Thursday," John said. "The end of the month."

Hennessy made a disgusted sound as he pocketed the notes. Still watching them he sidled toward the door, peering to see if a key was in the lock. He changed it from one side to the other, slipped out quickly and locked the door, confining them to the living room. They heard him hurry to the porch.

Mrs. Fleming would have dashed to the window, but John held her. "Don't go near. Not yet."

"Why not?"

John Fleming shook his head. "Don't let him think there's anyone to see a signal."

They listened to the car, roaring as Hennessy tested the engine. Then it moved out of the yard and as it changed gear for the hill, John dashed to the window. He dragged back the curtains and flapped them wildly.

"Look, sir."

Lewis pointed. The inspector saw the flutter of light in a window of Gorse Blossom.

"John Fleming's signaling, sir. It means Hennessy's coming out."

They peered down the dark valley. No sign of headlights.

The inspector said, "He's made a dash for it on foot."

"Or driving without lights," Lewis said.

They listened. Then they heard the car coming up. Its engine was striving.

"Stole the wrong car." The inspector smiled wryly. "You could hear that thing a mile off."

Gail watched them half turn a police car across the

road. Men waited. The dog was whining. For a while there were only the black shapes and the sounds of the climbing car. Then she remembered that Sam would be frightened by fighting. She led him up the slope, away from the road.

"Stand still," the inspector snapped.

Hennessy saw them as the car breasted the rise. He tried to swerve. A wheel blundered up the bank. The car tilted. He struggled to open a door, but as he forced it wide Constable Lewis was there and in the background a dog was growling.

It was the dog which finished Hennessy. He said, "Keep that thing off," not resisting as Lewis dragged him from the seat. He glanced over a shoulder to the dog as they searched him.

"Where you get the suit?" Lewis asked. "You'd need to grow six inches to fill that."

They were sneering at his height. Only five feet five inches. A small man to cause so much trouble. Hennessy glared, his vanity hurt.

"And this." Lewis found the food. "Where you get this?"

Hennessy grinned, nodding toward Gorse Blossom. Then they found the knife and the teasing went out of their voices.

"Where you get it?" the inspector snapped.

Hennessy shrugged. Let them work it out.

"Made it yourself, is that it?"

"Expect so, sir," Lewis said. "Hour after hour, week after week, all his spare time sharpening his lovely knife."

Hennessy didn't answer. He looked around at the bustle; police radios were sending messages to headquarters and the prison, the inspector was ordering a police car

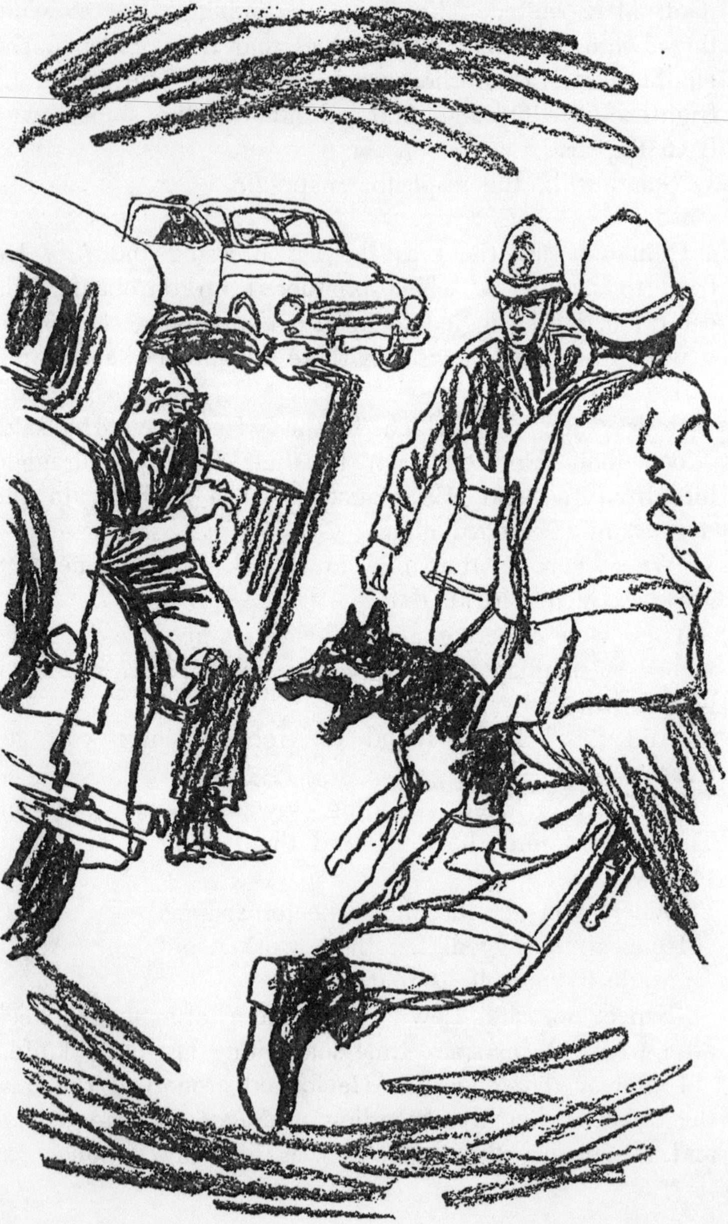

to Gorse Blossom while a constable prepared to drive back the stolen car. All this fuss for a little man. Not so little, Hennessy thought. He said, "I nearly made it."

Then he saw the horse and the girl. He thought about it, guessing the identity of the girl and realizing what had happened. He gave a little laugh, mocking himself because if he'd known about the girl and the horse, he might still be free.

Two constables pushed him toward the car which would take him back to the prison. He flashed another glance to Gail as he said, "You'd never have done it. Not without her."

"Get in," Lewis said.

Hennessy got in. "True though." He was mocking himself as well as them. "You'd never have got me if it hadn't been for the girl."

He peered through the window, appreciating the irony that one who was afraid of all animals had been beaten by one. Grimly he added, "And that flaming horse."

CHAPTER THIRTEEN

"You're famous," Gail said.

She folded the newspaper, showing Sam the headline, the columns of type; most important, the photograph. Sam looked down his nose at the photograph.

"Quite right," Gail said. "It doesn't do you justice. But you've never been so famous. Not even when you were winning races."

The photograph showed her standing beside Sam on a Dartmoor hill. The boy nearby was Rod. It seemed that one of her hospital paintings had been photographed and made real. Above it the big headline read: NIGHT DASH BY THIRD-FORM HEROINE ALERTS POLICE.

She didn't feel like a heroine. Her nose was red and stuffed because she'd been so long without shoes. The night grass had soaked her socks and the result was a cold in the head. That didn't sound like Florence Nightingale or Grace Darling or any of the heroines of history. It sounded like only one person in the world. Windy Fleming, cold feet all the time whichever way you looked at it.

"This is the best one," Rod said. "In the *Daily Mirror*."

She'd already seen it. She knew why Rod liked it best. It was the only photograph which didn't show his secret shame.

"There's nothing wrong with freckles," Gail said.

157

"Who's talking about freckles?"

"Well, there isn't," Gail said.

Rod made a disgusted sound.

"They can be quite handsome."

Rod made the sound again. Who wanted to be handsome?

"Or not exactly handsome." Gail realized she had chosen the wrong word. She fumbled for another. "More . . . more rugged."

Rod considered it.

"See for yourself."

Gail held out the *Daily Mail*. Rod looked a long time at the photograph, wondering if that was what rugged meant.

"This is the one I'll keep," Gail said.

She looked up the slope to her parents coming down. Each had an arm around the other and this was how she liked to see them. No more bickering about money or whether they could afford Sam or dared to let a girl ride him. Now they were close, closer than they had ever been.

"The television people," her father said. "Just rung up. They're sending over a film unit."

Gail remembered her nose. I hope this isn't in color.

"Rod must be in it, too," Mrs. Fleming said. "He wants to show everyone where you bit him."

"All of us in a group and Sam in the middle." John Fleming slapped the horse's neck. "That's how you want it, isn't it?"

Gail looked at her parents and at Rod, then up to the horse which had begun as a lonely dream. Yes, she thought, my father's right. That's exactly how I want it.

Vian Smith is a native of the Dartmoor country he writes about so vividly. During the seven years he served with the British Army in World War II, Mr. Smith wrote his first novel. After the war, he traveled a good deal and was a free-lance journalist. Vian Smith lives in Totnes, a small town in Devon, England, with his wife, his five children, and, of course, his horses, and devotes his full time to writing.